Ansley sped up. So did the dark SUV.

Are you really doing this? Both Maribelle and Harrison had made her question herself, hinting that she wasn't going to like what she found out. Telling her that they were only trying to protect her. What if they were right and she couldn't handle the truth?

She let up on the gas. The fear was still there. What if there was something horrible they were trying to shield her from? *Are you doing this or not?*

Ahead, there was a wide spot on the right, a turnoff onto a dirt side road on the left. The highway continued but in a curve, quickly hidden by the pine trees growing close to each side. There was no other traffic this morning on this two-lane highway outside the city. There was just her and whoever was in that black SUV.

HER BRAND OF JUSTICE

New York Times Bestselling Author

B.J. DANIELS

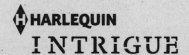
HARLEQUIN

INTRIGUE

If you have ever felt as if you didn't belong in your family and suspected that the babies were switched at the hospital or your parents stole you from your real parents, this book is for you.

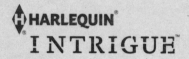

HARLEQUIN®
INTRIGUE™

ISBN-13: 978-1-335-58264-5

Her Brand of Justice

Copyright © 2023 by Barbara Heinlein

Recycling programs for this product may not exist in your area.

For questions and comments about the quality of this book, please contact us at CustomerService@Harlequin.com.

Harlequin Enterprises ULC
22 Adelaide St. West, 41st Floor
Toronto, Ontario M5H 4E3, Canada
www.Harlequin.com

Printed in U.S.A.

B.J. Daniels is a *New York Times* and *USA TODAY* bestselling author. She wrote her first book after a career as an award-winning newspaper journalist and author of thirty-seven published short stories. She lives in Montana with her husband, Parker, and three springer spaniels. When not writing, she quilts, boats and plays tennis. Contact her at bjdaniels.com, on Facebook or on Twitter @bjdanielsauthor.

Books by B.J. Daniels

Harlequin Intrigue

A Colt Brothers Investigation

Murder Gone Cold
Sticking to Her Guns
Set Up in the City
Her Brand of Justice

Cardwell Ranch: Montana Legacy

Steel Resolve
Iron Will
Ambush before Sunrise
Double Action Deputy
Trouble in Big Timber
Cold Case at Cardwell Ranch

Visit the Author Profile page at Harlequin.com.

CAST OF CHARACTERS

Buck Crawford—The cowboy and former highway patrol officer has a problem with trust.

Ansley Brookshire—All she wants to do is find out who she really is.

Maribelle and Harrison Brookshire—They were far from the perfect adoptive parents.

Colt Brothers Investigation—PIs James, Tommy and Davy have two mysteries to solve.

Sheriff Willie Colt—He wants to find out why his father was killed ten years ago.

Judy Ramsey—The waitress just needs money.

Penny Graves—The assistant just wants to help her boss and best friend.

Lanny Jackson—The Brookshire bodyguard is mean, thin-skinned and revengeful.

Gage Sheridan—Far from the perfect fiancé, is he in it for love or money?

Mayor Beth Conrad—She only wants the best for the Colt boys.

Chapter One

It wasn't the first time Ansley Brookshire had noticed
a black SUV following her after an argument about
finding her birth mother. It was, however, the first time
she'd seen her adoptive father leave his office to rush
home. What was different about this time? she wondered as she saw his driver pull into the estate. Her
mother—*adoptive mother*, she mentally amended—
must have called him. Which meant this time, because
she'd threatened to hire a private investigator, it was
serious. How far would they go to stop her?

The thought made her nervous—as if the black SUV
now tailing her wasn't enough cause for concern. It only
made her more determined. Her adoptive parents should
know that once she decided to do something, she did it.

Except that she'd never felt they knew her. She'd spent
most of her twenty-eight years feeling as if she didn't belong. An only child, she'd always been looking for someone who resembled her. Both Maribelle and Harrison
were blond, fair skinned with dark blue eyes. Then there
was Ansley, their only child, hair so dark it was almost
coal black, eyes a washed-out blue like old denim and

her skin olive instead of fair like her adoptive parents'. She'd never looked anything like them.

Now she knew why. Neither of her parents could have been responsible for her conception. At first she'd thought that she must have been adopted and they had just never told her.

But now she suspected that her whole life was a lie wrapped in secrets. When she'd asked for the truth, they'd lied to her. When she'd gone to public records to find details about her adoption, they weren't there. Had they stolen her as a baby? She still wasn't sure that hadn't been the case, even though Maribelle said it had been a private adoption and that's why she couldn't find any record of it.

Even private adoptions had records, which led her to believe that if she had been adopted, it had been illegal. Otherwise, she must have been stolen. Why else would Maribelle and Harrison be so adamant that she not look for her biological mother?

That's when she decided she would find out the truth no matter what.

Except the most recent "no matter what" appeared to be her father's bodyguard, Lanny Jackson, following her in the large black SUV he drove. What was it her adoptive parents were so afraid of her finding out? She felt a shiver of trepidation. Since her discovery, they'd done everything they could to keep her from learning the truth—or had they?

She glanced in the rearview mirror again. If they thought she could be intimidated, they were wrong. Maybe before all this began, she would have turned around, gone back to town to her apartment and waited for another day to follow the only lead she had as to who she really was. But she no longer felt safe even in her apartment. Since she'd discovered the big lie, she hadn't been able to shake the feeling that she was constantly being watched.

Never one to back down from a challenge, Ansley wasn't waiting another day. She finally had a lead. She wasn't going to put off chasing it. Even so, she'd tried again this morning to reason with her mother before she was forced to hire a stranger to help her.

That's why she'd gone to Brookshire Estate this morning, as it was commonly known, determined to give her mother one more chance to tell her the truth. Had she really thought that if she asked this time, it would be different?

Earlier she'd found Maribelle upstairs in the massive house where she'd grown up, standing in her huge walk-in closet, holding up one dress after another in front of her as she considered each in the full-length mirror. Clearly, she was getting ready for one of her many luncheons. Ansley had lost track years ago of how many boards her mother served on.

"What do you think, dear?" Maribelle asked, flashing her daughter a smile before returning to her image in the mirror. She hadn't seemed surprised to see her, even though Ansley had moved out of her room in the far wing right after high school and seldom showed up without calling. "I'm afraid the navy one says the wrong thing, don't you?"

"I've found a private investigative firm I'm going to

hire," Ansley said, getting right to the point. It had been something she'd decided after running into nothing but dead ends on her own. "I'd hoped it wouldn't come to this."

Her mother met her gaze in the mirror. This was far from the first time this discussion had come up since she'd stumbled across at least part of the truth.

Yet her mother looked genuinely perplexed. "Whatever for?"

"I need to know who I am."

"You know who you are," she said with a dismissive scowl. "Ansley Brookshire. Do we really have to go through this again?"

"I'm going to find my birth mother with or without your help." The look her adoptive mother gave her said it would be without her help, as usual. She recalled the fear she'd seen in Maribelle's eyes the first time she had confronted her after finding proof that she wasn't related to either of her parents.

"Why are you so afraid of what I'm going to find?"

"*I'm* your mother," Maribelle had said with finality. "I think the coral dress. It wouldn't hurt to stand out today," she said flipping her chin-length blond hair back as she returned her attention to the mirror.

Ansley moved to stand next to her until they were reflected side by side in the huge mirror. The contrast between them was startling. Maribelle was a natural blue-eyed blonde, a former beauty queen, tall and leggy. Ansley stood five foot five, with her obsidian-black hair, the palest of blue eyes and an athletic build. No one had ever believed that they were mother and daughter—not that her mother's social circle would have ever mentioned it, at least not to Maribelle's face.

How she'd come to live in this house as their daughter was only one of the many lies and secrets, she thought now. For years, she'd wondered why she was so different from her parents—and not just in appearance.

"I like the navy dress," she said to her mother, who smiled distractedly at her in the mirror.

"You would," Maribelle said. "You've always had that stubborn streak—just like your father."

"My birth father?" Ansley asked, making her mother's mouth form a thin, straight line of disapproval.

"What can I say to you to make you change your mind?" Maribelle asked with a sigh as she tossed the navy dress aside. "Your father and I were discussing buying a place in the Bahamas just this morning. We'd need you to do the decorating. You have such a good eye for that sort of thing. It would mean a lot of work, but I'm sure you can close your little jewelry shop for a few months while you're away."

Her *little jewelry shop*. Neither Maribelle nor Harrison had ever taken her jewelry making seriously—even when she'd turned it into a very successful business that more than supported her.

"I'm not closing my shop, and I'm not going to the Bahamas," she said. They'd already tried to buy her off. This was just another stalling tactic in the hopes she would change her mind. Or was it about giving them time to cover their tracks?

When she'd first confronted them with what she knew, Maribelle had offered her anything she wanted to drop this obsession. Then had begun issuing threats when bargaining and bribing didn't work. But since she was no longer dependent on them financially nor interested in inheriting their wealth, the monetary threats hadn't worked.

"You know I love you and appreciate everything you and my father have done for me," she'd said. They hadn't been a normal family—at least not like her friends' parents, who often ate together at the kitchen table in a roar of voices and laughter as everyone tried to talk at once.

Ansley had grown up eating in the kitchen with the cook and a nanny. She'd seldom seen her parents except in passing. They would give her a kiss as they left for this event or that. She'd thought when she was young that her father always wore a suit and her mother a fancy dress. She remembered the smear of her mother's lipstick on her cheek, the smell of her perfume lingering in the air as they rushed out into the night.

Not that she sincerely wasn't grateful for the advantages she'd had. But there had always been a hole in her heart she hadn't understood, as if she'd lost a missing piece of herself somewhere. Just as she had always felt there was some secret, something she hadn't been told, something important that had been left out.

She glanced in her rearview mirror again. The dark SUV was still back there. Harrison wouldn't pay his bodyguard to physically keep her from the truth, would he? She remembered seeing his driver pull in through the gate at the estate as she was leaving. She'd gotten only a glimpse of her adoptive father in the back with Lanny. Just from his expression through the tinted window, she'd felt a sliver of fear. For him to drop everything and come home at this time of the day... And now, if she was right, Lanny planned to follow her all day and night if that's what it took.

Ansley sped up. So did the dark SUV. *Are you really doing this?* Both Maribelle and Harrison had made her question herself, hinting that she wasn't going to like what she found out. Telling her that they were only trying to protect her from disappointment. What if they were right and she couldn't handle the truth?

She let up on the gas. The fear was still there. What if there really was something horrible they were trying to shield her from? *Are you doing this or not?*

Ahead, there was a wide spot on the right and a turn-off onto a side road on the left. The highway continued ahead but curved, quickly disappearing behind the pine trees growing close to each side. There was no other traffic this morning on this two-lane highway outside the city. There was just her and whoever was driving that black SUV.

Ansley put on her blinker to pull into the wide spot and turn around. She didn't have to do this today. Going by the estate had been a mistake. She should never have told Maribelle her plans.

As she came to a dust-boiling stop beside the highway, the black SUV sped on past. She couldn't see the driver's face, but from the large, bulky shadow behind the wheel, she knew she'd been right. It was Lanny Jackson, her father's personal bodyguard.

The moment he and black SUV disappeared around the curve, obscured by the trees, Ansley gunned her vehicle across the highway and onto the dirt road bordered by pine trees. She knew it wouldn't take Lanny long to turn around and come back. Ahead she saw yet another narrow dirt road to the right. She slowed just enough to take the turn and kept going.

She took the next road to the left and then one to the right. She had an idea where she was, so she wasn't surprised when she finally hit the paved two-lane highway miles to the north. She took it. The traffic was sparse in this part of Montana once you got out of the city.

No black SUV appeared behind her as she wound her way north toward Lonesome, Montana, and the only lead she had. She could see a spring squall building in the mountains. An omen that this was a mistake? She kept driving north, even though she knew that once Lanny reported that he'd lost her, there would be an even worse storm at Brookshire Estate.

Chapter Two

"This had better be an emergency, Maribelle," Harrison barked as he stormed into the house. "I was in the middle of an important meeting."

"You are always in the middle of an important meeting," she snapped back. She could see through the front window that his driver was waiting by his car, the engine running. Where was that obscenely large bodyguard of his?

"Maribelle?"

Any minute he'd be checking his watch, she thought bitterly. "It's about our daughter."

He groaned, rolling his eyes. "You told my secretary it was an *emergency*. I had Jackson follow her. What more do you want? Not only is it a waste of time and money, but also I now have no security other than Roger, and we both know how my driver would react in a real emergency."

She hated the way he talked down to her. It didn't help that he was nine years older. She'd been his child bride. He still treated her like a juvenile. And him acting like there was always someone waiting around the corner to rob him, kill him… She should get so lucky.

"This *is* an emergency. Ansley is hiring a private investigator to track down her biological mother." He stared at her, nonplussed. "She can't do that. We can't allow it."

With a sigh, he said, "Once she learned that we weren't her parents, this was bound to happen. So what if she finds her birth mother?" The question hung in the air. He narrowed his eyes. "What the hell have you done, Maribelle?"

She swallowed, feeling small and afraid, a feeling she abhorred. She was Mrs. Harrison Brookshire. Everyone wanted to be her. "I'll fix it. But I'm going to need Lanny's help—and money."

He shook his head. "You're the one who just had to have a daughter. At all costs. I let you take care of it, just giving you the money and staying out of the details, and—"

"Yes, I know all that," she said. She'd heard this lecture many times. He hadn't wanted a child and had made it clear from the beginning that it was her deal and not to involve him in any way. She'd had this picture in her mind of having a daughter just like her— matching dresses, people stopping them on the street to compliment them.

The fact that Ansley was nothing like her had been a huge disappointment. Nor had she realized how much work children were, even with nannies and boarding schools. "I might need a lot of money."

Harrison glared at her. "Since you have a purse full of credit cards and your own checking account that I refill monthly, I know you're not talking about money for new dresses or shoes or spa treatments or expensive trips." He looked as if he were grinding his teeth. For all the money the man made, he was crass and cheap about things that were important to her, and it annoyed her to no end. "How much, Maribelle? How much this time to undo whatever it is you've done?"

BUCK CRAWFORD CONSIDERED the weather for a moment before he parked his pickup in the alley behind Colt Brothers Investigation just off the main drag of Lonesome, Montana.

Snow in May? He'd awakened to sunshine only to have the clouds roll in, followed by rain, then sleet, and now he was watching the flakes fall, the wind whipping them around outside the warm cab of his pickup. Well, this *was* Montana, he reminded himself. Yet this winter was hanging on way too long.

Snowflakes had begun accumulating on his windshield before he snugged his Stetson down on his head, pulled his sheepskin coat around him and climbed out. With luck one of the Colts would have a pot of hot coffee going this morning.

Wind whirled icy flakes around him as if he'd stepped into a snow globe. He squinted through the blur of white as he hurried toward the back door of the narrow brick building that housed Colt Brothers Investigation.

But before he could reach to open the door, it was flung outward as a woman dressed in a long red wool coat came flying out. He glimpsed shiny black hair and startled pale blue eyes before he collided with her.

Instinctively he grabbed hold of her shoulders to steady her—and keep them both from going down. Their gazes met for an instant before she broke free and rushed down the alley, disappearing into the falling snow as she turned the corner and was gone.

Buck looked after her for a moment, still startled by the encounter—and what he'd seen in those eyes. Fear. As he considered going after her, he noticed that she'd dropped something in her hurried escape. Reaching down, he picked up what appeared to be a used envelope. The top had been sliced open, and it was now empty. It was addressed to Colt Brothers Investigation. There was no return address.

He turned it over and saw that someone had written what appeared to be a list of names and dates on the blank side. Was this something important that she needed? The writing was starting to blur from the wet snow landing on it. The woman long gone, he quickly tucked the envelope under his coat, opened the door and stepped in out of the cold.

As he entered the back of the Colt Brothers Investigation office, he pulled out the envelope and waved it in the warm air to dry it before the inked names and numbers ran. To his surprise, he recognized the names—all of them Colts, all the way back to his friends' great-grandfather Ransom Del Colt, who'd been a famous Western movie star in Hollywood back in the '40s and early '50s.

Their grandfather RD Colt Jr. had started his own Wild West show and traveled the world ropin' and ridin'. All the Colts had followed in their famous predecessors' footsteps, riding the rodeo circuit, including the brothers' father, Del, who later quit the circuit to start the PI agency.

It seemed the woman had picked up a discarded envelope and hurriedly written down not just their names, but dates associated with each. Why her interest in the Colt family? He didn't like the bad feeling this was giving him. Who was that woman?

Maybe more important, why, when she'd crashed into him, had she looked scared? He'd thought at that instant it was from the shock of not expecting to open the door and see a man there.

But after finding the envelope, he realized that something had happened inside the office that had made her look pale and shaky—and had her tearing out the door. Had one of the Colts told her something that had upset her? Didn't explain the envelope with their names and dates on it.

"James?" he called out. "Tommy? Davy? Anyone?" No answer. As he moved deeper into the main office, he kept seeing her face, those washed-denim blue eyes that had looked almost familiar, even though he would swear he'd never seen her before.

He stopped in the center of the main office. He'd been so deep in thought that he hadn't realized how eerily quiet the office was. Where was everyone?

Pushing open a door to one of the private offices, he saw with a start that it had been ransacked. Desk drawers stood open, and papers were strewn on the floor. A filing cabinet had been broken into.

"Hello?" he called tentatively as he pocketed the envelope and reached for the sidearm on his hip, only to belatedly remember he wasn't armed, no longer law enforcement. Nor was he a rancher raising rough stock for rodeos. Right now, he was in limbo, but those cop instincts had him on edge.

He moved stealthily through the building, checking each private office, finding them empty, all having been ransacked. As he did, he mentally kicked himself. He should have gone after the woman. All his instincts told him she had just brought trouble to Lonesome—and the Colt brothers. Just his luck that he was the first to cross her path. At least he could give them a description of her. Hopefully she hadn't taken anything.

Buck did wonder, though, what she'd been looking for as he pulled out his cell to call Sheriff Willie Colt, the oldest Colt brother. Before he could, James walked in through the front door holding a shallow cardboard box, the smell of cinnamon and sugar quickly filling the room.

He realized that James must have opened the office, then popped next door to the sandwich shop that his wife, Lori, used to own to pick up cinnamon rolls.

"What's going on?" James asked, glancing around as he carefully put the box down on the scarred old oak desk that had been his father's and now sat in the main office as reception.

"The offices—"

"They're ransacked," James said.

Buck nodded. "I think I might know who did it. As I was coming in the back door, a dark-haired young woman with these really pale blue eyes was rushing out in a hurry. It appears she had a look around before she left."

"Attractive young woman?" James asked, tongue in cheek. "Thanks for clarifying that."

"Seriously, she was…striking and somehow familiar." He frowned and saw his friend shaking his head.

"You make one heck of a witness. Any idea what she was looking for?" James asked as he quickly checked the offices.

"No idea, but she dropped this before disappearing down the alley." He handed James the envelope with the writing on it as the PI moved to the large old oak desk again. The family story was that the desk was the first thing Del Colt had bought used when he'd started Colt Investigations.

Del hadn't lived long enough to see each of his sons also leave the rodeo circuit to return to Lonesome, Montana. Three of them had taken over the PI business while Willie had turned to law enforcement, having recently been elected county sheriff.

"If I'm right and that's her handwriting on the envelope, it would seem she has an interest in the Colt family," Buck said as James sat down behind the desk.

"Let's try that description again," James said as he pulled out a notebook and pen. Buck drew up a chair and described her as much as he could remember to his friend.

"She doesn't sound familiar," James said, surveying his notes. The top of the desk was clean. He opened his desk drawer. "It appears she sorted through things, but nothing seems to be missing. She didn't take the business checkbook or the spare change I keep in here," he said, closing the drawer.

"She didn't seem like a woman who needed your spare change," Buck said almost to himself as he gazed at the wall with the posters of Colt ancestors. There was a framed movie poster of James's great-grandfather Ransom and numerous photos from RD Jr.'s Wild West show, along with action shots of Del's sons trying to ride bulls and broncs in local rodeos as boys.

"I take that back," James said with a curse as he followed Buck's gaze. "She did take something." He pointed to the wall where a small, faded rectangle showed where a framed photo had hung.

"Which photo was that?" Buck asked, frowning. He'd studied the wall many times but couldn't remember that exact print. Growing up helping his father and brother raise rough stock for rodeos, he'd been as infatuated with the sport as anyone. It was something he and the Colts had always had in common.

"It was one of the four of us out on the ranch," his friend said. "It was my dad's favorite of us boys."

Buck remembered it now, the brothers looking as if they'd been wrestling in the dirt, their jeans as filthy as their faces, Western shirts torn and askew, the knees of their jeans caked dark with mud, their cowboy hats pushed back on their dark heads with all four of them grinning from ear to ear.

"You might have a problem," Buck said. "There was something about the woman I couldn't put my finger on, but I felt as if I'd seen her before. More of concern, she looked shaken when she came flying out the back door. Whatever she found, it scared her."

ANSLEY WAS STILL in shock by the time she reached her SUV parked down the block on Lonesome's main drag. She climbed in, hurriedly started the motor and turned on the wipers to brush away the snow that had accumulated in the short time she'd been gone. But she couldn't drive right now. Her hands were shaking too hard, her heart a thunder in her ears as she fought back tears.

She couldn't believe what she'd just done after finding the investigation office unoccupied. She'd known whoever had unlocked the door must have just stepped out. They would be back soon. She'd planned to have a seat and wait, but she'd been so nervous that she couldn't sit. Instead, she'd noticed the wall of photos and posters and had been drawn to it.

She'd found herself searching the faces. Her eyes had widened in surprise, shock and then alarm. Even now she couldn't believe what she'd been thinking. What she was *still* thinking—that the answer had been staring her in the face? She'd grabbed a used envelope off the large reception desk and a pen and had furiously written down names and dates as she'd tried to make sense out of what she was seeing.

The envelope. She looked around for it now, searching her coat pockets and groaning as she realized that she must have dropped it in her hurry to escape. She'd been frantic to get out of there after she'd heard a noise upstairs. It had sounded as if someone was rummaging around up there. That's when she'd noticed one of the office doors ajar and had seen the mess. Someone had done this, and now they were upstairs and could be coming down the steps at any moment.

She'd taken off out the back, realizing that when one of the Colts came back, he'd think she'd made this mess. It was bad enough that she'd impulsively taken a framed photo off the wall. What had come over her?

She dug again for the envelope she'd written on, hoping she hadn't dropped it. But given the way she'd torn out of there, she wasn't surprised that she must have. What would the Colt brothers do when they returned? Call the sheriff? What about the cowboy she'd crashed into on her way out?

As she pulled her hand from her empty coat pocket, she realized that she had cut her finger enough to make it bleed. When she'd taken the photo? She vaguely remembered catching her finger on the nail. Pulling out a tissue from the glove box, she frowned as she wiped away the blood, then turned up the heater, feeling chilled in a way that had nothing to do with the Montana spring weather. The wipers were barely keeping up with the falling snow, and yet to the south, at the end of the main street, she could see blue sky on the horizon.

She should get out of town. People could already be looking for her—and not just the men from Colt Brothers Investigation. She thought of the cowboy she'd nearly knocked down. If he hadn't grabbed her… They'd looked at each other, but only for an instant. She'd half expected him to chase after her and had been relieved when he hadn't. She told herself that she wouldn't recognize him even if she saw him again.

With the snow falling, the flakes so large and lacy, she could barely see across the street. She shouldn't drive until she got control of herself. Maribelle was right about one thing—she wasn't herself. Her actions today proved that.

Guilt nibbled at her. She'd been relieved when she found out that Harrison and Maribelle weren't her birth parents. She'd always felt not just alone and lonely, but like an outsider. Her life might have appeared charmed, since it appeared that she'd never wanted for anything. And yet she'd ached for what she'd thought of as a real family. Her true family, she believed now.

As her heart rate began to drop back to normal, she felt her resolve returning. She wouldn't turn tail and run. Not now, especially. The answer *was* in Lonesome. A few days ago, she'd tracked down her original nanny and questioned her. If there had been any evidence of where Maribelle and Harrison had gotten her, she figured Gladys Houser might know.

Gladys had been in her fifties when she went to work at the estate, a matronly spinster who seldom smiled. She'd been her nanny until Ansley was five and entered preschool.

Now over eighty, Gladys had been reluctant to talk to her. She'd pursed her lips when questioned and said, "I don't like talking about former employers."

"Please. Anything you can tell me might help me find my birth mother."

As if seeing how badly Ansley needed to know the truth—and that she wasn't going to stop until she did—

the former nanny had said she couldn't help, because she knew nothing about the adoption.

She said she'd heard about the employment opportunity through a friend who thought she'd be perfect for the job because she'd taken care of newborns before. She'd gone to the estate, met with Maribelle and been told that she would be living in the wing farthest away from the couple so their sleep wouldn't be disturbed.

"It was clear that Mrs. Brookshire wasn't pregnant, so I was to wait until the baby arrived," Gladys had told her. "A few days later, Mrs. Brookshire came in with a newborn. She carried you into the nursery and put you down in the crib and left. You were crying, and your diaper needed changing. I took over and spent every day with you until you were walking. Mrs. Brookshire hired a second, younger nanny to keep you busy during the day. I stayed in the employment until you went to preschool, taking care of you at night and on the other nanny's days off."

"What about how I was dressed or what I was wrapped in the first time you saw me," Ansley had asked. "Any clue as to where the adoption had taken place?"

She had waited, seeing that Gladys knew something. Just from what the nanny had said, she hadn't been a fan of Maribelle and her parenting.

"You were wrapped in a knit blanket. It had a tag on it that read 'made with love,' but quite frankly, the knitting was very amateurish," she said, turning up her nose.

"As if a teenager might have made it?" Ansley had suspected her birth mother might have been too young to keep her. Gladys had shrugged. "What happened to the blanket?"

"Mrs. Brookshire told me to dispose of it in the trash, along with a plastic bag with some disposable newborn diapers and what appeared to be clothing someone had bought for you." Ansley had felt her heart sink. "I couldn't bring myself to throw any of it away. Someone had obviously cared. I took it to a friend whose daughter could use the clothing and the blanket. I found a receipt in the bottom of the plastic bag. The yarn had been purchased in a store in Lonesome, Montana, some months before Mrs. Brookshire brought you to the house."

Ansley had started to ask about the family who'd taken the blanket that her birth mother might have knit herself, but Gladys had already been shaking her head.

"The family moved. I have no idea what happened to the blanket. I'm sorry. I shouldn't even be telling you this much."

"What color was it?"

"Pink. A pale pink. But she'd also bought enough yarn for a blue one as well, according to the receipt."

"As if she didn't know if she was having a boy or a girl," Ansley had said, more to herself than to Gladys.

She had thanked her, tears in her eyes as she'd left. Her biological mother had loved her. Why else had she knit her a blanket "made with love"? But why had she given her up? If she had willingly.

Ansley had followed that thin thread of a lead to Lonesome. When she'd researched online, she'd seen that there was a private investigation business in the small Western town. She'd told herself she would hire

them to find her birth mother. That had led her to Colt
Brothers Investigation.

After years of yearning for someone who resembled her, everything had gone as planned—until she'd
walked into the PI office and had seen a wall full of
photographs of people who looked so much like her that
she'd been swamped with emotion. That's when she'd
heard the noise upstairs and panicked, grabbed the small
photo of the boys from the wall and run.

All the time, she kept thinking, what if Maribelle
and Harrison had been right? What if she couldn't handle the truth?

Chapter Three

Maribelle fumed. It was clear that she couldn't stop Ansley. Nor could she depend on Harrison to do anything. His idea of help was throwing money at the problem. Too busy with his empire to run, he'd always told her to handle things and then complained about the way she'd done it. Had he gotten her a baby daughter? No, she'd had to do it herself. Just as she was going to have to take care of this matter herself.

She made the call, not surprised that the woman's landline phone number hadn't changed in twenty-eight years. "I need to see you."

A cough, then a gruff "Who is this?" in that husky voice she remembered.

"Don't even pretend that you don't know," Maribelle snapped, wondering what she'd been thinking to ever get involved with this woman. As much as she hated to admit it, Harrison had been right. Getting a baby had been a bad idea. Worse, now that baby had grown up and was threatening to destroy everything Maribelle had accomplished in life. If what she'd done ever came out...

She thought of the night she'd met Judy Ramsey, one of the servers working for the catering service at a party she attended. The woman had been on her knees in the bathroom heaving up her guts. Maribelle had just hoped it wasn't something she'd eaten in the kitchen that the caterer had brought.

"Morning sickness," the woman had said as she'd flushed and risen.

One look at Judy Ramsey and she'd seen an opportunity. "You don't sound happy about the pregnancy." Judy had merely mugged a face in answer as she'd rinsed her mouth out under the faucet at the sink. "Is it a girl? Or a boy? Or is it too early to tell?"

Judy had studied her for a moment. "Girl." That had been the magic word—and the answer to Maribelle's longing for a daughter. It had only come down to how much money Judy would demand.

"We need to meet," Maribelle said now and heard the woman cough again. In the background it sounded like the television was on one of those daytime stories. She silently groaned to herself. She could imagine the woman's face, the greed in those beady eyes—she could see her calculating how much a meeting would net her. The thought of giving this woman another dime turned her stomach.

"Is that so?" There was a teasing, mocking quality to her tone that made Maribelle grind her teeth. Had she already heard that Ansley was searching for her?

"Meet me on the old river highway at that motel and café tomorrow evening. Seven. Don't be late." She disconnected before she could change her mind. Harrison would definitely not approve of what she was planning to do. But then again, he seldom approved of what she did. Worse, she might make matters worse.

But she had no choice. She stepped to her walk-in closet–slash–dressing room, opened the bottom drawer and reached in the far back, past her expensive negligees, to the box she kept there.

Drawing it out, she opened the box and took out the gun, even though she told herself that she had no intention of using it. The gun had been her father's. He was the one who'd taught her to shoot. She'd never told Harrison about it. Nor did he know she knew anything about weapons. There was so much about her he didn't know. Lack of interest, she thought. He'd taken one look at her long legs and her long blond hair and big blue eyes and had seen everything he'd wanted in her. Which had worked in her favor. He'd married the woman he thought she was, the fool. He never would have made such a mistake when it came to business.

She tucked the firearm into her designer leather shoulder bag next to the envelope of cash Harrison had grudgingly removed from the safe in his study. That done, Maribelle walked into her closet to go through the process of deciding what to wear tomorrow. It was very important to choose the right outfit—maybe especially to meet a woman you were probably going to have to kill.

SHERIFF WILLIE COLT was on a mission of his own after returning recently from a case out in Seattle. His life had been a whirlwind since then. He'd fallen in love and gotten married—something he'd thought he would never do—to a very attractive attorney in Seattle who'd stolen his heart. Now he and Ellie were building a house on Colt Ranch.

He'd also found a girl's gold necklace in the wrecked pickup his father had died in almost ten years before.

While he'd never been this happy, or this busy, he was still determined to find out what had really happened to his father the night he died. When he'd originally joined the sheriff's department as a deputy, he'd thought it was temporary. The only reason he'd taken the job was to try to get to the truth about his father's death. Del had died when his pickup had apparently stalled on the tracks. Struck by the train, he'd been immediately killed and his pickup totaled. The sheriff back then had closed the case, declaring it an accident.

But Willie and his brothers had never believed that. Unfortunately, he was never able to find any evidence that proved otherwise—even as a deputy in the sheriff's department.

Instead, what had happened was that he realized that he liked law enforcement—just not the sheriff at the time. So he'd run for the office against him—and won. It hadn't stopped him from looking for answers. After returning from Seattle, he'd gotten lucky and found his father's pickup in a wrecking yard, miles from Lonesome. On the floorboard behind the seat of the king cab, he'd found the small, tarnished gold necklace with the name *DelRae* engraved on it.

Since then he'd been even more obsessed with finding what had happened that night on the train tracks.

His father had warned his sons about crossing where there were no bars, no flashing lights, and yet Del had gone to that very spot and been hit by a train that night almost ten years ago. It made no sense. Where had he been going on that dirt road that led up into the mountains? Had he been meeting someone tied to one of his PI cases?

The only clue they had—other than the necklace—was a report called in to the sheriff's department from an anonymous source who said she saw Del Ransom Colt arguing with a woman in front of a downtown bar in Lonesome not long before he died on the tracks. Unfortunately, the sheriff at the time hadn't gotten the woman's name. The crooked sheriff also could have made up the story to make it look like Del had been coming from the bar and was drunk.

Online, Willie had found there were dozens of Delraes but no DelRae, the way it was spelled on the necklace. Since he had no idea how old DelRae had been or would be now, he had nothing to go on.

His cell phone rang. He saw it was his brother James and quickly picked up. Things had been relatively slow at the sheriff's department lately. It wasn't quite tourist season in Montana. Kids were still in school for a few more weeks. The only excitement was the upcoming high school graduation, which brought out most of the town since so many people in the county were related.

This latest snowstorm had a couple of deputies out because of fender benders, but other than that, Willie had found himself digging through the mountains of paperwork that went with the job.

"Something strange happened here at the office this morning," James said without preamble. He went on to tell Willie what had been taken and how Buck Crawford had seen a young woman escaping.

"That's all that was taken?" the sheriff asked. "Just a photograph of us?"

"I know that doesn't seem important, but that was Dad's favorite. I want it back."

Willie smiled at the anger he heard in his brother's voice. "And this criminal mastermind was a woman, a young, good-looking woman, given Buck's description. Sounds like he was taken with her."

"I'm serious. Maybe you could come take fingerprints, *Sheriff.* We have an envelope we believe she wrote on, but I figured the desk and drawers would produce a better print."

He couldn't believe what he was hearing. Before he could argue, James said, "Davy just found some blood. She must have cut herself on the nail when she took the photo. We need to run DNA on it."

All this over a stolen photo, even his dad's favorite? "I think you're overreacting, but I'll be right over. Don't touch anything else." He disconnected, chuckling to himself. James knew that most people's fingerprints weren't in the national database—not to mention how few people even had their DNA on file.

But if it would make his brother feel better… And it was a break-in and something had been stolen and he *was* the sheriff.

BUCK CRAWFORD LEFT the Colt brothers to their work. He was at loose ends. An injury had forced him to leave his job as a state highway patrolman. While he'd healed, at least physically, he didn't want to go back to being a patrolman. Nor did he want to join his father and brother out on the ranch raising rough stock for rodeos. He didn't know what he wanted to do with the rest of his life—and he was only thirty-five. Except thirty-five often felt old. His future appeared to be a long, dark, endless tunnel—unless he took the advice of the psychiatrist he was required to see after his injury and let it go. He chuckled. If only it was that easy, he thought.

As he walked down the main drag of Lonesome, he knew he had to make a decision about his life. He'd never been in this state of mind before. Almost dying did that to a person, he thought. But he knew it was much more than that. He'd been told that he had trust issues.

The snow had let up, and as usually happened in the spring in Montana, the sun peeked out through the clouds. What snow had stuck was now melting, the icy water running down the street.

Like a lot of small Montana towns, this one had that Old West look with the usual: a courthouse, post office, jail, bank, an old movie theater, a hardware store, a clothing shop, grocery, several cafés and an assortment of touristy shops that sold everything from T-shirts and Montana curios to quilt fabric and antiques.

There was a damned good steak house outside town, near the fairgrounds. If a person wanted more, they could drive to Missoula or one of Montana's other larger cities. There weren't that many. Buck had seen enough of cities. When at home on the ranch, he seldom even drove into Lonesome.

But today he'd been more restless than usual. If he hadn't been, he realized, he wouldn't have come into town today. He wouldn't have run into the woman fleeing the PI office. He'd been thinking about her when he noticed a white SUV pull out of a parking space up the block and head in his direction.

He caught a glimpse of the woman behind the wheel. His heart rate kicked up. She wore large sunglasses, and while she didn't look in his direction, he was positive it was the same woman. The collar of her red wool coat was turned up.

As she passed, he tried to read her license plate number under the road grime but only got the last three numbers. He wanted to run back to the alley where he'd left his pickup and give pursuit, but knew he couldn't reach his truck quickly enough and catch her, since she was headed for the highway out of town.

Nor did he have any business chasing after her. He reminded himself that he was on an extended leave from the highway patrol—a tenuous position at best. He was just a plain old civilian without any authority to chase down the woman. Best to leave chasing this particular criminal to the Colts.

Yet, as he watched her white SUV disappear down the highway, he couldn't help wanting to go after her. Just as he couldn't help being intrigued. What had she been looking for in the Colt office? More important, what was her interest in the Colt family? Wasn't that what worried him the most? He felt protective of his friends. They'd gotten him through some tough times in his life. He owed them.

He texted James with the three numbers he'd gotten off the license plate and a description of the vehicle's make and model.

THE SHERIFF CONSIDERED the spot where the missing framed photo had been, bagged the envelope in question, attempted to get prints off the desk drawer handles and had his lab tech take a blood sample for a DNA test. Then he stopped to study the photos and posters on the wall. He'd looked at them a million times growing up, but he still enjoyed studying them. The Colts had one hell of a legacy, he thought with no small amount of pride.

For so many years, growing up just outside Lonesome, he and his brothers had had free rein. His father hadn't believed in running roughshod over his sons. No wonder a lot of people in these parts called them "those wild Colt boys." Willie knew his brothers thought their childhood had been magical and wouldn't have changed it for the world. As the oldest, Willie had known a darker side, one he'd made sure his brothers had been spared.

His gaze fell on a photo of his father on the back of a bronco just moments before it had dumped him in the dirt. The look on Del's face was priceless. Willie knew that kind of wild happiness. He'd felt it many times while on the rodeo circuit—and recently having fallen in love.

Now he wondered—as he had ever since finding the girl's necklace in his father's wrecked pickup— had there been someone in Del's life after he lost his wife and his sons' mother? If so, he'd kept it a secret, which made the girl's tarnished gold necklace and their father's death even more of a mystery. As he studied his father's photo, he promised himself again that he wouldn't give up until he knew what had happened that night on the railroad tracks.

"Thanks for doing this," James said as he joined him. "I can't imagine what the woman was looking for. Why would she steal a photograph of the four of us boys as kids?"

"Because we were so dang cute?" Willie joked.

His brother pulled a face. "I'm serious. It's…weird." Willie couldn't argue that. "Buck just called. He saw her leaving town. He got a partial plate number on her white SUV. Said it's a newer Escalade and the plate was framed with a dealer's name in Bozeman."

Willie took the information his brother had jotted down and promised to get back to him. He didn't hold out much hope on fingerprints or DNA coming back with a hit. But they just might get lucky with the license plate numbers and vehicle description. He couldn't help being curious about this female mastermind, he thought with a chuckle.

Chapter Four

After picking up a few supplies for the ranch, Buck headed out of town. He'd thought about sticking his head in at Colt Brothers Investigation to see if they'd learned anything about the woman but changed his mind, knowing that one of them would have called if they had any new information.

He was only a half mile out of town when his stomach growled. He realized he should have at least gotten something to eat since it was still a long way to the ranch. Ahead, he saw the sign for the steak house. Several cars were parked out front. One thought of the restaurant's burgers and fries and he couldn't help himself. He swung in.

It wasn't until he'd parked that he noticed a white SUV parked on the side of the building that looked a lot like the one he'd seen the dark-haired woman driving.

His heart bumped up a few beats as he got out and walked over to it. Same model SUV, same framed license plate from Bozeman. He pulled a glove from his coat pocket and wiped off the plate so he could read all the numbers. Same last three numbers he'd given James Colt.

It was her.

He looked up, hoping she wasn't watching him from one of the front windows as he headed for the door. As he caught a whiff of something frying, the hot-grease smell making his stomach growl even louder, he considered how he was going to handle this.

It wasn't until he pushed open the door and saw his mystery woman sitting in a booth by the front window that he made up his mind. She looked lost in thought, with what appeared to be a cup of coffee growing cold in front of her. It appeared that's all she'd ordered. He wondered how long she'd been sitting here. If anything, she looked paler than earlier and possibly just as scared. *Striking* was the only way he could describe her.

As he approached her, he warned himself that she was going to be as skittish as a wild horse—and even more challenging to get a rope on if he handled this wrong. She'd had her hands in her lap but raised them to the table, palms down. Her hands were pale, with finely shaped fingers and perfect nails painted a demure pale pink. But what caught his eye was the glint of the ring. He hadn't noticed it when they'd collided with each other earlier in the alley.

Now, though, he couldn't miss the pear-shaped diamond on her left ring finger. It was large enough to put an eye out. The woman was engaged.

He felt a strange mix of emotions. Of course, he'd been attracted to her instantly in the alley. She was beautiful, and he hadn't been that close to a woman in quite a while now. He swore he could still smell the faint hint of her perfume on his sheepskin jacket. For so long, no woman had even made him turn his head. So why the interest in this one? Just to get the Colts' photo back?

Chuckling to himself, he hoped that's all it was. It would be just like him to be drawn to a criminal, he thought with self-deprecation. Yet he couldn't deny her allure, which, upon seeing her again, was stronger than ever. Who was this woman?

For just an instant, he tried to talk himself into walking on past her table and letting her be. *This is not your rodeo.* But he knew himself too well. He would always regret it. He wanted to know her story. He was also the only one who could positively identify her as the woman he'd seen running scared out of the ransacked office.

Now he had her dead to rights.

But as he neared the table, his common sense argued again for him to let it go. Let *her* go. She was trouble. All his cop instincts, the ones he thought he'd also packed away for good, wouldn't let him. Damned if he wasn't still a lawman at heart.

His fear was that this disturbingly attractive woman with her big blue eyes was a con artist—and the Colt brothers were now her marks.

"Excuse me, Miss."

Ansley hadn't heard the cowboy approach her table. She looked up, startled, but even more alarmed when she recognized him.

"Mind if I join you?" He didn't wait for a reply as

he slid into the booth across from her and removed his Stetson. He set it on the booth seat beside him before returning his gaze to her.

She'd thought that their encounter had been so brief that neither of them would remember the other. Clearly, she'd been wrong. She remembered the blond hair that curled at his neck under the cowboy hat, the intensity of his blue-gray eyes, even the feel of his large, strong hands on her shoulders as he'd steadied her in the alley. Several days of stubble added to the strong jawline, but it was the way he looked at her that welded her to her seat and stole what little breath she had managed to take.

After a few moments, she finally found her voice. "I'm sorry. I was just about to leave." She reached for her purse and coat on the seat next to her. Earlier, she'd stopped at the steak house needing a cup of coffee, needing time to think. She'd figured she was far enough out of Lonesome that she was safe. Wrong again.

"I think we should talk."

There was nothing threatening in his tone. She turned back to him, studying him as intently as he was her. She saw now that his hands were calloused, the hands of a workingman. His voice was deep and yet gentle, almost soft. He was handsome in a rough and rugged way that she thought she would never have found appealing.

For a moment, she felt lulled into believing that this man meant her no harm. But given the way they'd first met... Common sense told her to get out of the restaurant, out of town. Even if she hadn't had the shock of her life earlier, she didn't feel up to a confrontation with this cowboy.

Yet wouldn't it make her look guiltier if she walked out now? Worse if she ran? She replaced her purse and coat on the seat and, taking a breath, let it out slowly as she waited. *Hear him out. See what he has to say.* They were in a public place. What was the worst that could happen? Well, he could be trying to keep her here until the law arrived to arrest her.

"I didn't come in here to give you a hard time," he said quietly, as if sensing her uneasiness. "Actually, I'm hungry. You don't mind if I order something, do you?" He really wasn't going to drag this out, whatever it was, was he? She started to tell him that she needed to be going, but he cut her off. "I appreciate you not pretending that we didn't cross paths earlier in the alley."

Out of the corner of her eye, she saw the waitress headed in their direction. Ansley knew that she could use the distraction to leave. She didn't think this man would try to stop her. She didn't think he would make a scene. If he planned to have her arrested, he would have already called law enforcement, wouldn't he? She glanced out through the window, but she didn't see any patrol cars.

She could feel him watching her. He was expecting her to make a break for the door. She sat back, determined to prove him wrong, reminding herself that it wasn't as if she'd broken into the PI office. Nor had she been the one to ransack the place.

If she hadn't impulsively taken something on the way out, she would have been able to claim her innocence. Not that she probably would have been believed. If she hadn't been so nervous earlier, she might have realized that someone had ransacked the offices before she'd walked in. Or realized that she wasn't alone—that whoever had done it was still in the building.

She considered him for a long moment wondering what he wanted from her. Maybe more to the point, what he planned to do, since he'd caught her leaving Colt Brothers Investigation earlier—and while innocent of ransacking the offices, what she'd stolen was in her shoulder bag on the seat beside her.

"Whatcha goin' to have, Buck?" the young gum-chewing waitress asked, all smiles as she reached the table.

"Hey, Susie. I'll have a burger and fries," he said and looked across the booth at Ansley. "How about you? Have something more than coffee. I hate to eat alone. You don't want to just sit here and watch me eat."

She felt Susie's quizzical gaze on her. Buck had made it sound as if they were old friends who had purposely met here today for an early lunch.

"Bring her the same," Buck told the young waitress and waited a beat to see if Ansley was going to argue before he added two colas to the order.

"Sorry for being presumptuous," he said after Susie left. "But I really do hate to eat alone, and I thought you might be hungry. Thought maybe you'd had enough coffee, since I suspect you've been sitting here for a while."

Ansley studied him with growing interest and foreboding. Who was this cowboy? Had he followed her here? She was still so shaken by what she'd seen in the

PI office that she wouldn't have noticed. Was he stalling until backup arrived? Surely this man wouldn't need to wait for backup.

"We haven't properly met," he said with a smile that lit up his handsome face but didn't quite meet those eyes. "Buck Crawford. My family ranches outside town. Raise rough stock. For rodeos. I tried to ride most everything we raise. Thus the scars." His smile wasn't quite as bright, giving her the impression he had other scars—those harder to see. There was something beguiling about him.

Under other circumstances she might have appreciated this cowboy's attention.

But she was still too shaken by what she'd found inside the PI office, let alone the shock of running into this man on her way out. Him showing up here had her feeling even more off balance. He would want an explanation, and right now she didn't have a believable one.

The smell of frying grease was making her nauseous. She couldn't imagine eating a bite. Why hadn't she gotten up and left the minute he approached her? She needed to put an end to the suspense.

"What is it you want from me?" She was surprised how calm she sounded even as her heart raced.

"The truth might be nice." Funny, she thought, she'd come to Lonesome in search of the truth. "But how about just your name to start." He was no longer smiling, but his tone was gentle, like his demeanor. "First name will do if that's all you want to share."

She took a breath and let it out. His apparent kindness was making this harder for her, and yet she was sensing an undercurrent of suspicion. He said he raised stock for rodeos, but his manner felt more like that of a cop.

Ansley swallowed, giving herself a moment. Buck Crawford wasn't wearing a sheriff's department uniform, but he could be off duty. Nor had he come here to arrest her, or he would have already done it.

"It's Ansley," she said, wondering if she was making a mistake even talking to him. Normally, she was levelheaded, both feet firmly on the ground, but this day had knocked her catawampus. She felt as if she couldn't trust herself—especially around this cowboy. "Ansley Brookshire."

"Brookshire?" he repeated, frowning. "Brookshire Oil and Gas?"

Everyone in Montana knew the name, because her adoptive father's name turned up in more than just the oil and gas business. Harrison Brookshire invested in anything that made money—and quickly slapped the Brookshire name on it.

She could feel the cowboy's speculative look. No doubt he was wondering what would have brought her all the way to Lonesome—let alone the Colt Brothers Investigation office.

"You're probably wondering what I was doing at the PI office this morning," she said, her voice not quite as steady. She'd never imagined when she came to Lonesome, Montana, to hire a private detective that she would walk into the office and see all those photographs of people who looked like her.

But it was that one photograph of the Colt brothers—

their faces so much like her own at that age—and their happy smiles… Impulsively, she'd taken the framed photo. Why had she never realized that finding her biological parent might mean finding a family that had grown up entirely without her? A family that had been happy and full of siblings, something she had yearned for her whole life?

"You seemed upset as you were leaving," Buck Crawford said, encouraging her to continue.

Upset? She felt a distraught laugh rise up her throat. This cowboy already thought the worst of her. She didn't need to make it any worse by laughing and not being able to stop. Her emotions were too close to the edge right now. *Upset?* She'd been shocked, gutted, elated, terrified, furious, heartbroken. Her emotions had run the gamut—and still were.

"Yes," she said as she fought back the erratic emotions. "I *was* upset." Even as she thought about it, she reminded herself that she was probably wrong. It could just be a coincidence that the boys in the photo looked so much like her at that age—sans the grins. She'd come to Lonesome looking for family. Her only lead had brought her to Lonesome, Montana, and Colt Brothers Investigation.

But had she really found them? Or was she as delusional as Maribelle thought she was for doing this?

Susie came back with their lunches then, balancing the plates in her hands before putting them down, then pulling ketchup, mustard and hot sauce from her large apron pockets with a flourish. "Anything else I can get you?"

Buck Crawford looked to Ansley. She shook her head and thanked Susie, and the young woman left.

In the silence that followed, Ansley said, "You're a cop."

He seemed surprised that she thought that before he said, "I used to be. Now I'm just a rancher, like I said."

"Then I'm confused by your interest in what I was doing in Lonesome this morning," she said.

"I've known the Colt brothers all my life. I won't let anyone hurt them." He softened his words with a smile. "Let's eat while it's hot." He dived in with relish, but she'd heard the threat, seen the granite-hard glint in his eyes. She didn't doubt he meant it.

She told herself that she wouldn't be able to eat a bite even as she picked up her burger. Out of the corner of her eye, she watched the man across the table. He wasn't just trying to protect his friends. Somehow this was personal for him.

Chapter Five

Willie couldn't believe that they'd actually gotten a decent print from Colt Brothers Investigation office. Even more surprising was that when they'd run it through the system, they'd gotten a hit. "Lanny Jackson?"

His deputy beamed. "Got a rap sheet as long as my good leg. Mostly when he was younger, but we're looking at assault, intimidation of witnesses, breaking and entering… He's done little time behind bars, though. Probably where the intimidation of witnesses comes in."

"What was he doing in Lonesome?" Willie said, more to himself than to Deputy Chris Fraser.

"Been employed for seven years as a personal bodyguard by Harrison Brookshire," Chris said.

"*The* Harrison Brookshire?"

"The one and only."

Willie shook his head, surprised that a man like that would employ a criminal as his bodyguard. Then again… "I don't get it. We know a woman matching the description Buck gave us was in the office. Could Jackson's print be an old one?"

The deputy shook his head. "Doubtful. James said

no one has been in that office for a while, with Davy on a case down in Wyoming."

Leaning back in his chair, Willie considered this. Buck had said the woman had looked scared as she'd rushed from the office. What if she wasn't the one who'd ransacked the place? What was she doing here to start with? And which one of them had stolen the photo of the four Colt brothers?

He felt a chill. A man like Harrison Brookshire didn't get where he was without bending a few rules—hiring Jackson as his bodyguard seemed proof of that. He told himself that Brookshire might have hired Jackson to rehabilitate him. If so, it didn't appear to be working. So what had the man been looking for in the office—and had he found it?

"As for the blood that was found where the photograph was taken," Chris was saying, "we're waiting on the DNA test results. Think they were in it together?"

Was it just a coincidence that while James was next door getting cinnamon rolls, two people with no connection were waiting in his office—one looking for something, the other…? That's just it. They had no idea what the woman had been doing there. Yet they had an envelope with their names on it that she'd dropped after running into Buck.

Willie had to admit it made him worry now that they knew Lanny Jackson was involved—not to mention that Harrison Brookshire might be, too. "I'm just wondering who took the photo from the wall—and why."

BUCK HAD TOLD the truth—he really had been hungry. He put away the hamburger and fries in record time.

Not that he hadn't been studying the woman across from him as he ate. He put her in her mid- to late twenties. Well-dressed, she exuded confidence even though he'd caught up with her. She was a Brookshire, after all. Knowing she had her daddy's money and power behind her would give any young woman confidence.

He'd been trying to get a read on her beneath the veneer of privilege. He was better with wild horses then women, he thought with a silent chuckle. Always had been. Thus his downfall, he thought.

Still, he got the feeling that she didn't have it together as much as she pretended. He'd seen fear in her eyes when she'd come tearing out of the Colt Brothers office. She'd been running from something. Weren't they all, he thought as he pushed away his plate, glad to see that she'd eaten some of her burger and fries. He'd always found that getting some food under his belt seemed to steady him. Right now he needed steady, and he suspected she did, too.

"You don't have to tell me what you were doing in the office earlier," he said as he leaned back in the booth and settled his gaze on her. If she got up and left, he wasn't going to try to stop her. He had her license plate number, the make and model of her car—and if she was telling the truth, he had her name, a name that would make even their new sheriff think twice about taking this questioning any further.

She pushed away her plate as well and straightened in the booth to look at him. She had the palest blue eyes— even more dramatic because they were fringed with dark lashes. He still couldn't shake the feeling that they'd met before. But he wouldn't have forgotten a woman who looked like this, he was sure of that.

"I came to Lonesome to find my birth mother," she said, her voice stronger than earlier.

"Why Lonesome?"

"I didn't have much to go on, only a receipt that was found in a bag of baby clothes, according to my original nanny." She looked down at her hands resting on the edge of the table for a moment, then back up at him. "I had decided that I was going to hire a private detective to find her. Colt Brothers Investigation seemed the logical place to start."

He nodded. "The only PIs in town."

"When I found the office door open, I decided to go in and wait. I was looking at the photos and posters on the wall when I heard someone upstairs. It sounded as if they were frantically looking for something. I panicked and left."

His gaze locked with hers. "But why take the framed photo of the Colt boys?" He saw her swallow before she dragged her eyes away.

"You're going to think I'm delusional. I certainly do," she said quietly. "That photo, the boys, their faces at that age… There is a photo of me on the mantel in the house where I grew up." Her gaze came back to his. She swallowed before she said, "Our faces. We look identical. Except for the grins." Her voice broke. "I came to Lonesome looking for my biological mother, hoping to find my true family, and when I saw that one photo…" Her voice broke. "I realized that I could have found them."

There it was, he thought with a start. Why she looked

so familiar. She was right. The washed-out denim blue of her eyes, the almost coal-black hair. But while the Colts were handsome in a rugged way, this woman was a dark-haired beauty.

Could it be true? He told himself that there had to be dozens, hundreds, maybe even thousands of people that she might resemble. What were the chances she was related to the Colts? If that was really why she'd taken the photo.

"So you're thinking they could be cousins? Even…" Brothers? The thought shocked him. "How old are you?"

"Twenty-eight."

"When's your birthday?"

"Fourth of July. At least that's what I was told and what it says on my birth certificate, which I now know isn't original."

Same age as Davy almost to the day?

He could feel her staring at him.

"Like I said, I know it sounds delusional," she said.

"You must have been shocked." He was shocked at what this could mean—if true. But if this was some kind of scam…

Those big blue eyes filled with tears. "I *was* shocked. I can't describe how I felt knowing that I could have grown up with them if my mother hadn't given me up. That is, if I'm right."

He saw now why she'd written down the names and dates on the envelope. She was trying to figure out how she fit in—if she did. "Do you still have the photo you took from the wall?"

She looked embarrassed as she reached into her

shoulder bag lying next to her on the booth seat and brought it out. Carefully she laid it on the table between them and their dirty dishes.

Buck picked it up, remembering the Colt brothers at this wonderfully innocent age. What wild boys they'd been. Del had raised them alone after losing his wife. Maybe *raised* was the wrong word, he thought, unable not to smile, since he'd been only a little older than Tommy and had often come home just as dirty and scraped up as the Colt brothers after a day with them.

"I see the resemblance," he said looking from the photo to her, wondering what she'd been like as a girl. He quickly reminded himself that he was jumping to conclusions, just as she had. Until they had some kind of proof...

He tried to hand the photo back, but she didn't take it right away, so he set it down where she had earlier.

"I just wanted to compare it to the photograph of me at about the same age," she said. "I wanted to see if they match as closely as I think they will. I wasn't thinking or I could have simply taken a photo with my phone. It was just impulsive, something I'm usually not."

"You should keep it for now. Just hang on to it. It has sentimental value to the Colts."

She hesitated, but only for a moment before she picked it up, studying it before she put it back into her purse. She seemed to be waiting to see what happened next.

What *did* happen next? Buck cleared his voice. "I'm not one to usually dispense advice, but if I were you, I'd come back to Colt Brothers Investigation office with me. You can tell them what you told me. A DNA test will quickly clear up whether or not you're related to the Colts in any way. If you are…" He tried to imagine how his friends would take the news. If she was their half sister, then that would mean that Del Ransom Colt, the father they'd idolized, had a child they'd never known about.

He reminded himself that he was putting the cart before the horse. All this was speculation. Or worse, if this woman was running a con. For all he knew, she wasn't even the daughter of Harrison Brookshire. Maybe nothing she'd told him was the truth. It wouldn't be the first time a woman had deceived him.

"If you're related," Buck said. "I suspect the Colt brothers will want to find out the truth about your birth mother as badly as you do."

"You sure they won't have me arrested?"

"For stealing a photograph?" He shook his head. "Even if you aren't related, I think you'd be smart to hire them as you originally planned. If your biological parent has a connection to Lonesome, they'll find it—and her." He could see her making up her mind. If she hedged, then it would certainly appear that nothing she'd told him was the truth.

"All right." She nodded. "I've come this far. I need to see this through."

He wasn't quite sure, surprised it had been that easy. "Good," he said as he picked up his Stetson from the booth seat. "Let's take my truck. I'll drive you back to your car afterward just to make sure you're safe."

"You don't trust me."

Chuckling, he said, "I've been told I have trust issues."

She cocked her head, a half smile on her lips. "But I should trust you?"

He shrugged. "Up to you. I'm just trying to help."

"Why is that?"

"You need help, and right now, I'm kind of in between."

"In between what?"

He grinned. "Jobs. Just in an odd place in my life that I never thought I'd ever be. It's a long story and not one I'm going to bore you with. You want a ride? Great. Otherwise…"

Chapter Six

James had figured he'd never see the mysterious woman Buck had run into leaving the office earlier—or the missing photograph—again. So he was more than surprised when his old friend walked into the office with the woman shortly after noon.

He'd just hung up from a phone call with Willie about a hit on the fingerprint found in the front office. He was trying to get his head around what the sheriff had told him when they walked in.

Buck had described the woman well. He saw at once why his friend had been taken by her—she was strikingly pretty. As he offered them both chairs, he quickly assessed her. Somewhere in her late twenties, educated, nicely dressed and with an air of privilege about her.

Once seated, she introduced herself. Ansley Brookshire, daughter of Harrison Brookshire. That got his attention. The fingerprint had belonged to Lanny Jackson, bodyguard to Harrison Brookshire. So she hadn't come alone?

Yes, she had been in the office earlier. Yes, she had taken the photo, which she pulled out of her expensive shoulder bag but didn't offer to return. Yes, she had left in a hurry. Her story was that she'd heard someone upstairs searching frantically for something and hadn't noticed before then that the offices had been ransacked. So she didn't know her father's bodyguard had been in the building ransacking the offices? Was that possible?

"I want to hire you to find my birth mother," she said in conclusion. "I have little to go on, other than a receipt for yarn bought in Lonesome months before I was born. It's what brought me here, and since you are the only private investigators in town…" James saw her glance at Buck, who nodded, before she turned back, swallowed and seemed to brace herself. "Also, I think I might be related to you."

Okay, that he hadn't seen coming. There was a resemblance, yes, but… "In what way?"

She shook her head. "I think I might be your sister. Half sister. Or at least cousin?"

James was at a loss for words. "Based on what evidence?" A receipt for yarn in a bag with baby clothes from a shop in Lonesome?

"You could do a quick DNA test," Buck said. "Should answer that question, right?"

"DNA test results aren't quick," he said, already knowing that Willie had taken the blood sample and was having the lab run it. It wouldn't take much to see if it matched any of the brothers. Willie's DNA was already in the system because of his job. "We are already running your DNA. When you took the photo, you cut yourself. I put a rush on it." There was no way she was their half sister, was there?

She didn't seem surprised or worried that they might have the results of the DNA test sooner rather than later. He glanced at Buck. He knew his old friend too well—Buck wasn't completely convinced. But then, the former law officer wouldn't be in a situation like this one.

What Buck didn't know about was the girl's necklace Willie had found in their dad's wrecked pickup with the name DelRae engraved on it. Hard not to jump to conclusions. He knew when Willie met this woman and heard her story, he would instantly think the same thing now whirling in James's own mind. Except this young woman's name wasn't DelRae. There might not have ever been a connection between the necklace and their father. All this could be conjecture.

But that didn't mean that she wasn't the little girl who'd been given the necklace. Or that she wasn't Del Ransom Colt's daughter—and their half sister. Wasn't that why he was hesitant to take on this case? Because he didn't want to believe his father had had another child? Or worse—that his father had had another child he'd kept secret?

Yet James couldn't brush this under the rug just because he didn't want to believe it. "Like Buck said, there is one way to prove it. We'll know when we get the DNA results if we're related. In the meantime…" He studied the woman. Damned if she didn't resemble him and his brothers. "I'd like to see the photo of you when you were about the same age as me and my brothers in the one you…borrowed from the wall."

"I'll get it and bring both of them back to show you.

You'll take my case?" she asked. The hope in her voice alone should have decided for him.

"Your parents told you that you were adopted?" James asked.

She shook her head. "I found out by accident. I was looking for something in my father's study and I found a letter from a local physician that made it clear that neither of my parents had been capable of conceiving a child and that adoption was recommended. The physician said he would put them in touch with an agency if they were interested."

"Did he mention the agency?"

"I already checked. They didn't go through an agency," she said. "When I brought it up with my... adoptive parents, they refused to talk about it. From what I've been able to find out, they didn't go through any of the legal adoption procedures. I've searched adoption records. As I understand it, Maribelle passed me off as her own after lying that it had been a home birth. How else could she have gotten me a birth certificate?"

James thought about that for a few moments, then asked for her date of birth. He couldn't hide his surprise. He supposed the Brookshires could have managed it given their financial situation. "Do you have anything else to go on besides the receipt that brought you to Lonesome?"

She shook her head but then hesitated. "There is one thing I should tell you. My adoptive parents are so adamant about me not finding my birth mother that they have tried to buy me off, threatened me and even had me followed."

"*Followed?* Did they know you were coming here?"

"My mother knew. I suspect she called my father, because he came home from work as I was leaving. But I was being followed before that. I lost the tail, though."

"Do you know a man named Lanny Jackson?" he asked and saw her expression change.

"He works for my father as his…bodyguard. He's the one who followed me when I left the estate."

"His fingerprints were found in the front office this morning."

Her eyes widened, and for a moment, he saw his brother Davy. Hell, maybe she *was* their sister. "He'd been following me earlier, but I was sure that I'd lost him."

"Why do you think your adoptive parents don't want you learning the truth about your birth mother?" James asked.

"It was a private adoption, they said. But I suspect it was illegal. I've even thought that they might have stolen me. I suspect they're afraid I'm going to learn the truth and that it will come back on them." She frowned. "If Lanny was in your office looking for something earlier…" Her blue eyes widened again. "Then he reached Lonesome and your office *before* me." She shook her head. "I have no idea how that was possible. I looked up Lonesome on my computer and found your office…" Her voice trailed off, and a knowing, shocked look came into her expression. "What if they haven't just had me followed? Is it possible they've been somehow tracking everything I do?"

"It's possible. Jackson might have been trying to find a connection to your birth mother and our PI agency," James said. "He could have just been fishing." Or he could have been sent to destroy any evidence he found. James couldn't bear the thought of a cover-up by his own father. If there was a cover-up, he should have found evidence of it by now, wouldn't he have?

"We'll take your case," he said, realizing that he needed to know the truth as much as she did. He could see that his longtime friend Buck looked worried as well. If he took the case, he would be going up against Harrison Brookshire's power—and his muscle. That alone made him want to take on the case, even though he knew it would be dangerous.

"Where can I reach you?"

She gave him her cell phone number and her apartment address. "I'd like to keep this photograph of the four of you until I retrieve the one of me from the house where I grew up. If that's all right with you. I want to compare them. I promise to bring it back."

James nodded, although a photo wouldn't prove anything. The DNA sample now being processed would tell the tale. He needed to know what it was her adoptive parents didn't want her to find out. He told himself it could be merely the possible fallout if an illegal adoption came to light. There could be any number of reasons the Brookshires didn't want their daughter to find out the truth.

He studied the young woman, unable not to see the

resemblance—and just as unable not to be worried for her. She didn't look afraid. She looked angry and even more determined. "You're sure you want to go forward with this?" he had to ask.

"Yes," she said with authority. She reached for her purse. "You'll want a retainer—"

"I also need a copy of your birth certificate, Social Security number and any other pertinent information to the case." She nodded. "You're sure you're twenty-eight, born on the Fourth of July?"

"I'm not sure. According to my former nanny, my adoptive mother brought me home on July fifth—the day after I was allegedly born. So it definitely wasn't a home birth."

"I'm sure you realize that your father…adoptive father and mother…have a powerful reach. But they might not be the only ones who don't want the truth to come out." He hated to even mention this but knew he had to. "Your birth mother might not want to be found." He saw her surprise.

"Maybe she doesn't want to be found, but I really don't believe she would harm me to keep me from finding out the truth," Ansley said.

Had she really not considered this? He admired her optimism, but at this point they had no idea what they were going to find. "If you're determined to do this… I'd be very careful if I were you."

If Lanny Jackson was any indication, she was already in danger. What if her birth mother really didn't want to be found? Also, if any of this were true and she was related to them, then this case could rewrite their family history. If she was their half sister, then the news could be devastating to their father's memory.

Meanwhile, they were all now—including Buck Crawford—in the crosshairs of whoever was determined to keep the truth about Ansley Brookshire's birth a secret.

BUCK TOLD HIMSELF to walk away. He'd done what he could by bringing her back to the PI office. James and the rest of the Colts would take it from here.

Yet as he drove her out of Lonesome toward the steak house, where she'd left her vehicle, he didn't want to walk away. Nor did he want to dig too deep into why he felt that way. It wasn't just because he was worried about this woman, although he was.

Ansley had been quiet after they left James. Was she having second thoughts? He doubted it, given the set of her jaw. "If you're still determined to go back to your adoptive parents' house for that photo, why not stay in Lonesome and go in the morning?"

Ansley seemed to consider. "It has been quite the day."

Buck nodded. "And a long drive back to Bozeman. Often best to sleep on it."

She smiled. "I won't change my mind."

"I can see that. But I agree with James about the danger. Isn't there someone who could go with you tomorrow to collect the photo you're after?" *A witness*, he thought but didn't say.

Meeting his gaze, she said, "I really doubt that's necessary, but I can call my fiancé." She was silent for a few moments. "I know I haven't handled this well, so I can understand why you'd be concerned about me. But I'm much stronger and more capable than I look. I've just had a shock today and I'm not myself."

"I don't doubt that you're plenty strong, but like you said, you've had a shock. Also, I've known James Colt all my life, and if he's worried that you're in danger, then there is reason for caution. You said you were planning to come back to Lonesome once you got the photograph, but I'm betting you plan to show the photo of the Colt brothers to your adoptive parents." Ansley didn't deny it. "That would be dangerous for everyone concerned—including the Colts."

"Dangerous? Over a photo?"

"There's a lot more at stake here, I suspect," he said as he pulled in next to her SUV and put the truck into Park before turning to her. "Lanny Jackson was sent to Lonesome to the PI office. This time he was searching for something. Next time, he could be sent to make sure the Colt brothers don't find out the truth. I know you want to compare the photos for your own assurance. But it will prove nothing. Once the DNA test results come back—"

"You sound as if you're hoping I'm wrong and that the results will prove it," she said, locking her gaze with his.

He couldn't deny it. "I just know that if true, it opens a whole can of worms for my friends, who want to believe the best about the father they lost almost ten years ago."

"You're saying they would rather believe the best of him than know about a half sister?"

He shook his head. "If you're related, the Colts will welcome you into the family. They'll move heaven and earth to find out the truth for you—even if it tarnishes the memory of their father. I'm saying that it will be hard to watch them go through that, but nothing will stop them."

"I don't want to hurt them," she said quietly. "Is it wrong to hope just the opposite of you? I've always dreamed of a family, but I never imagined I might have four brothers—half brothers."

"It's not wrong, and I have to admit, the first time I laid eyes on you, there was something so familiar, I would have sworn that we'd met before. I can see the resemblance." The more he was around her, the more he could see so much of the Colt genes in her, but he kept that to himself. Maybe because he hated to see her get her hopes up as much as he hated to see his friends go through this ordeal. "Never doubt that they will make you part of the family if you really are Del Ransom Colt's daughter."

She looked out at the shadows forming in the nearby pines. "When I realized I was adopted, I thought maybe there was someone out there like me." She shook her head. "I know. I can't let myself think that until we have proof. In the meantime, I need to compare the photos. But..." she added with a smile as she turned back to him, "you're right. It can wait until tomorrow."

"The motel in town isn't too bad for a night," Buck

said. "Then tomorrow, do me a favor and take your fiancé with you to the house. What can it hurt?"

"Thank you. For everything." Opening the pickup door, she stepped out, met his gaze for an instant and then closed the door and walked to her SUV. He sat, engine running, as she climbed into her vehicle and pulled away.

He watched the SUV until it disappeared down the road, and then he followed at some distance back to town, telling himself he was a damned fool. This had nothing to do with him. He'd done all he could. He needed to back off.

But he couldn't. Just as he couldn't shake the feeling that this woman didn't realize what she'd set in motion and where it might lead.

And here he was getting in deeper.

Remember the last time you got involved with a woman in trouble? He had the scars to prove it, including the one that ran diagonally from just below his breastbone down to where the knife had plunged into his torso.

It wasn't until she reached the motel and entered the office to check in that he turned around and headed home to the ranch. He doubted he was going to get any sleep.

Chapter Seven

"We have a new client," James said, then cleared his voice. He could feel his brothers' gazes on him, expectation in their expressions, just as he could feel their growing concern. It wasn't like he called a meeting every time they had a new client. Also, Willie was here. As the county's newest sheriff, Willie had little interest in new PI clients.

"Why aren't we going to like this?" Willie asked, cutting to the chase as usual.

James raised his head, not surprised his oldest brother was the one to ask. Willie probably already knew where this was headed. It was what made him a good officer of the law. "Her name is Ansley Brookshire, and yes, her father is the Harrison Brookshire."

"I guess we won't have to worry about getting paid," Tommy said and then must have realized neither Willie nor James smiled at his joke.

But before he could speak again, Davy piped up from the Zoom connection on the open laptop nearby, "What am I missing?"

"Buck came back by with our new client earlier.

We talked." He didn't say that Buck had made a convincing argument. If they didn't take the case, Ansley Brookshire would hire another agency. The truth was going to come out, one way or another. "She's looking for her birth mother. I told her we would take the case, since she suspects the woman might have lived or still lives in Lonesome."

He saw Willie cross his arms impatiently as if to say, *spit it out.* "What aren't you telling Tommy and Davy?"

"Here's the thing," James said. "Ansley Brookshire thinks she's related to us. She thinks she's our half sister." The dead silence that followed didn't last long.

From the monitor, Davy asked, as if he'd heard wrong, *"What?"*

"You can't be serious," Tommy snapped. "Our half sister?"

"Seems you left out something. This is the woman who ransacked your offices and took the photo of the four of us, right?" Willie asked.

"She ransacked our offices?" Davy demanded.

"There's more to the story," James said quickly. "I'll get you all up to speed as soon as I can. In the meantime, we have a blood sample that has been sent to the lab for testing. Once we have that, we'll know if she is even related to us."

"How old is this woman?" Willie asked.

James looked down at the information he'd taken from her, even though he didn't need to check her age. He'd never forget what she'd said. "Twenty-eight." She would have been conceived about the same time as

Davy—if her birth date was correct. But he didn't point that out. He didn't have to.

"It's bull," Davy snapped. "Dad would have never cheated on our mother." Davy had never met their mother. James hardly remembered her and doubted Tommy did, either. She hadn't been well, in and out of hospitals. She'd been like a ghost in their young lives, here and then gone. "I don't have time for this." Davy was gone in a flash of the screen.

Willie reached over and closed the laptop before sitting down on the edge of their father's huge oak desk with a resigned sigh. "What does she have for proof?"

"She's gone to collect a photograph from when she was about the same age we are in Dad's favorite photo." He saw Tommy look to the wall and open his mouth, no doubt to ask where it was. "She's going to bring both photos back. She says that when we see the resemblance…"

"Sounds like a scam," Tommy said. "I just can't see what she hopes to gain. Can't be money."

James was looking at his older brother, waiting. Willie had to have jumped to the same conclusion that he had. "Her adoption apparently was private and not necessarily aboveboard. Tommy, I want you to look into adoptions. You should know that her adoptive parents are dead set against her finding her birth mother—let alone, I would think, her birth father."

"You think she's DelRae," Willie said as if it was a no-brainer.

"Truthfully, I don't know what to think," he said as Tommy swore and reached into the bottom drawer of their dad's desk. He pulled out the blackberry brandy and the paper cups. His hands were shaking.

"Dad would have told us," Tommy said.

"Unless he didn't know until the night he died," Willie pointed out. They'd all heard about the alleged confrontation with a woman in front of the bar that night. The eyewitness said the woman had thrown something at Del. He'd stooped to pick it up as the woman stormed away. Otis Osterman, the sheriff back then, hadn't gotten the eyewitness's name. Since Willie had found a little girl's gold necklace in their father's wrecked pickup, they'd assumed that's what his father had picked up from the ground that night—if any of the story was true.

James swore. "If the child was his, how could he not have known about her? There's the damned necklace that we're all assuming he bought for her. Also, we have only a crooked sheriff's word that a woman saw Dad and another woman arguing on the street that night."

"But what if it's true? Maybe it wasn't Otis concocting the story to insinuate that Dad was drunk," Willie argued. "The coroner said he'd had a drink but wasn't over the legal limit."

James couldn't believe that they were having this same argument without any evidence. "We don't know that this woman even exists. According to Otis, the alleged woman said Dad staggered to his pickup. Otis has always wanted us to believe that Dad had been drunk or on drugs and that's why he'd stopped on the railroad track with the train coming."

"The autopsy report doesn't lie," Willie snapped. "Whatever happened that night, it wasn't because he was drunk or on drugs. Did this Ansley Brookshire say anything about a necklace?"

James shook his head. "Of course, I didn't say anything about it. We'll keep that to ourselves. Once the DNA test results come back… The whole issue might be moot."

"Or not." Tommy handed them each a paper cup. They usually didn't drink the blackberry brandy except to celebrate. There was nothing to celebrate now. Unless finding out your father might have had an affair the same year your mother was dying was cause for celebration, even if you got a half sister out of it, James thought.

"You think it might be true?" Tommy asked after he'd downed his brandy.

"She resembles us, no doubt about that." James looked at Willie. His brother had been convinced for almost ten years that their father's death had been foul play. He'd just never been able to prove it. Was it possible this woman, Ansley Brookshire, held the key that would finally reveal the truth?

"I want to meet her," Willie said after finishing his brandy and balling up the cup in his large fist. He tossed it in a perfect arc. It rimmed the trash basket for a moment before going in.

"You'll all get the chance," James told them. "She's coming back with the photo. At least she said she was. Buck called earlier to say he talked her into staying at the motel in town for the night and going down tomorrow to get the photo. He's worried about her going to **the Brookshire Estate by herself.**"

The brothers shared a look. It was only Willie who mumbled the obvious. "Damn fool. I thought Buck had learned his lesson."

AFTER A NIGHT of weird dreams, Ansley awakened worried. Had she done the right thing hiring Colt Brothers Investigation? What if she really was their half sister? It all felt like too much for her to grasp. One moment she was filled with excitement at the thought of finding the missing part of her life, of having siblings, of having a family that felt like a real family.

So why was she scared? Because it was clear to her that James Colt was hoping she was wrong. Maybe Buck didn't know the Colts as well as he thought. What if they wanted nothing to do with her? She couldn't imagine finding the family she'd wanted her whole life, only to have them push her away.

Was this why her adoptive parents had tried so hard to talk her out of her search? Maybe they knew something she didn't. What would they do when she told them that she'd hired Colt Brothers Investigation? She thought about what Buck had said. If she told her adoptive parents, would they harm the Colts? They'd tried bribing her, threatening to disown her and even having her father's bodyguard follow her. But she didn't really believe they would do anything beyond that, did she?

A shudder moved through her. She reached for her phone. That was the problem: she had no idea what the secret of her adoption was—or how harmful the truth might be to any of them. "It's Ansley," she said unnecessarily as her fiancé answered her call.

"Where are you?" Gage sounded impatient. "I've been trying to reach you." She glanced at her phone, surprised to see that he'd called a half dozen times and apparently left her messages. She remembered turning her phone off last night, exhausted and desperately needing sleep. She'd been glad that Buck had talked her out of making the drive until this morning.

"I had my phone turned off," she said as she looked around for her purse before heading to her SUV parked outside her motel room. "Why? What's going on?"

BUCK HADN'T SLEPT WELL, EITHER. With his life at loose ends, he worried that he was getting too involved in Ansley Brookshire's quest to find her birth mother. Why else was he up so early and now parked across the street from the motel?

Her SUV was still parked in front of one of the rooms. He hoped she'd gotten more sleep than he had. He also hoped that she'd changed her mind about driving all the way back to Bozeman to pick up a photo at her adoptive parents' house. Given the time, he was beginning to think maybe she had changed her mind.

But just then, he saw her come out of her room and head for her vehicle. She was on the phone. He slid down behind the wheel a little. The last thing he wanted was for her to think he was stalking her. He watched her climb in and start the SUV.

Was she still going back for the photo? If so, he worried what would happen when she showed the one of the Colts to her adoptive parents. If they were really that determined to stop her from finding her birth mother, they certainly weren't going to be happy about her thinking she was related to former rodeo cowboys turned private detectives, he suspected.

As she pulled away, he caught movement out of the corner of his eye. An older-model pickup pulled in after her. Buck sat up, realizing that the truck had been idling across the street. He hadn't noticed anyone behind the wheel and didn't get a good look as the truck went by, sun glaring off the windshield.

Buck told himself that he was just being paranoid. The driver of the truck hadn't been watching the motel and wasn't now following Ansley out of town.

But as he made a U-turn, he swore. He couldn't seem to shake off the suspicious cop in him as he watched the driver of the pickup match the white SUV's speed as both headed south of town. Damned if the driver wasn't following her. Only, whoever it was, they weren't someone her wealthy adoptive father had hired, his gut told him. Not in that old pickup.

No, unless he was mistaken, this was someone else with a dog in this fight.

Ansley held the phone away from her ear for a moment. Gage sounded angry. "You didn't get any of my messages?"

Obviously not, Ansley thought as she drove south out of Lonesome. "Well, I've called now. What's wrong?"

"I came by your apartment last night. Your SUV was gone."

"I stayed in Lonesome."

"Lonesome?" Gage demanded. "So this is about that

ridiculous quest of yours? Your mother called me, frantic with worry about you. She asked if I knew where you'd gone. Of course, I didn't. The fiancé is the last to know, apparently." She'd stopped telling him about her search for her birth mother after he'd made it clear that he thought it was a bad idea.

"She knew where I went. I told her yesterday morning when I stopped by the house."

"She was beside herself with worry, saying that you'd argued and then taken off. She feared in your state of mind that something terrible had happened to you."

Maribelle, beside herself? Not likely, she thought. "I'm fine."

"Did you really threaten to hire a private detective? Ansley, you're breaking their hearts, and mine, too. What is it you think is missing in this fairy-tale life of yours?"

They'd had this conversation before. Of course, he couldn't understand. He knew who his biological parents were and could see no reason for her to find hers. He also really believed that she'd lived a magic life just because of the Brookshires' wealth. He'd said many times that he would gladly trade places with her, even though his father owned a thriving business and did well financially. Just not as well as Harrison Brookshire, but then, who did?

"I really don't want to have this argument again," she said. "Anyway, I'm driving. I'm on my way to the house now. I thought you might want to meet me there. I'm picking up a photo of me when I was five."

"A photo? Whatever for?"

She really didn't want to get into it with him, and yet she couldn't help being excited. "There's a chance I've found my family, and the photo will help prove it." She described the small, framed photo that sat on one end of the mantel at Brookshire Estate. Maribelle liked the shot because Ansley had been in a pretty dress, her hair fixed with a bow, her cheeks pink, her blue eyes staring straight ahead at the photographer. She looked precious, Maribelle often said. No grin, but if Ansley remembered the photo as well as she thought, then she did look exactly like the Colt brothers at that age.

"You're joking. You want me to leave work to pick up some photo of you?"

"I don't think there will be trouble, but I could use the emotional support, if nothing else."

"I'm at work. I can't leave. I don't understand you." She could imagine him brushing back his perfectly coiffed head of salon-blended blond hair in frustration. It made her think of Buck Crawford and his imperfect, darker sun-streaked natural blond shade.

"I know you don't understand. Never mind. It was just a thought," she said, shoving away the reminder of Buck irritably. It wasn't fair to compare Gage and the cowboy. They were nothing alike in so many ways. "I'll talk to you later." She disconnected and took a deep breath, letting it out slowly. Was it Gage who'd changed? No, she thought. It was her. As he said, he didn't understand why she had to do this. When they'd met, she'd been the daughter of Maribelle and Harrison Brookshire. The owner of a successful jewelry business, a seemingly contented young woman with her life on a fairly straight, paved highway ahead of her and no speed bumps in sight.

They'd met at a conference at Big Sky. Gage's father had a beverage distribution company in Bozeman but did business all over the Northwest. Gage had taken over the business after his father fell ill and died, and he made no secret of the fact that this wasn't what he wanted to do the rest of his life. He couldn't sell, though, without his mother's agreement. So far, he hadn't been able to convince her.

Ansley thought about how he'd been impressed that she'd made a viable business out of designing jewelry using Montana gems. He'd asked her out soon after Big Sky, and they'd started dating and he'd been the perfect attentive boyfriend. It hadn't taken him long to ask her to marry him. He'd proposed after a dinner at the Brookshire Estate in front of her parents—all before she'd discovered they weren't her birth parents. She'd seen their delight at her engagement to Gage. Her father thought Gage had promise.

Recently, though, her fiancé had become more unhappy with his family business. Then Ansley found out that she was adopted and had become determined to find her birth mother, alienating herself from her adoptive parents—and Gage.

"If you don't stop, they are going to disown you," Gage had said. "Where is that going to leave us?"

Us. Wasn't that the moment when she began to realize that he wasn't as enamored with her as he'd claimed? He'd fallen in love with the Harrison Brookshire empire and what that much money could do for his life. Not that she could blame him. He wasn't the first boyfriend who'd had dollar signs in his eyes.

She pushed the thought away to consider the Colts. What if they really were her family?

The driving time passed quickly. As she neared the exit that would take her to the estate, she realized she would have to face her mother alone. More than likely her father would be at work—as usual. She doubted he would come home early again, even if Maribelle called him when Ansley arrived at the house. Still, she couldn't imagine that her adoptive mother would object to her taking the photograph.

As she turned into the drive to the estate, she didn't notice the older-model pickup behind her that pulled over just outside the gate. Ansley was thinking about the framed photograph she'd taken from the Colt Brothers Investigation office—and the one she wanted to compare it to. What would Maribelle say when she saw how much Ansley resembled the Colts in the photo?

Her heart thumped against her ribs. Was she about to find her family? Or blow up her entire life, including Gage and their engagement with it?

BUCK SAW THE pickup pull over as Ansley's white SUV turned into a paved drive that led up through the pines to a monstrous brick structure. He'd been debating how to handle this after impulsively following both the pickup and Ansley. He had no doubt that this was the Brookshire Estate she'd mentioned.

True to her word, she'd gone straight there to get the photograph that in her mind would prove everything.

Meanwhile, Buck needed to deal with whoever had been following her. He pulled in front of the truck, blocking the driver's quick escape. Jumping out, he headed for the driver's side of the truck. As he approached, he could see a shadow behind the wheel wearing a Western hat pulled low, though he couldn't tell if it was a man or a woman driver.

Before he could reach the driver's side door, the pickup's engine revved, just as he'd feared. The truck roared backward, then jumped forward, almost clipping him as it sped away. All Buck could do was get the license plate number. It wasn't nothing, but he didn't get the satisfaction of seeing who was driving that pickup and finding out why the person had been following Ansley Brookshire.

Back in his own truck, he considered chasing down the pickup or heading back to the ranch or going on up to the house. He had a bad feeling about just leaving. Ansley had said she wouldn't go alone, but it darned sure looked as if she was doing just that.

He knew he'd be welcomed like ants at a picnic, but that had never stopped him before, he told himself. *You should just let this go. This isn't your business. Don't be a damned fool. She isn't going to appreciate you following her down here.*

Buck realized he'd never been good at taking advice, even good advice, from anyone, let alone himself. He had become involved the moment the woman rushed out the back door of Colt Brothers Investigation and into his arms.

Starting his truck, he drove up the paved road to

the house. There was a gate, but it was open. Fortunately, there was no guard station, except there were plenty of security cameras and what appeared to be a laser beam across the road. He drove through it, realizing that someone now knew he was coming. Ahead he could see Ansley's SUV was parked outside. There was no sign of her. Or anyone else. Yet.

Chapter Eight

Tommy did a crash course in adoption in Montana by calling the county attorney. He told Attorney Frank Edwards a little about the case he was working on—a woman had discovered she had to have been adopted because neither of her parents could have children. They'd confessed it was true, and now she was interested in finding her birth mother.

"There are a lot of hoops to jump through in any legal Montana adoption—lots of steps that end with two hearings," Edwards said.

He explained that Ansley's adoptive parents could have done a direct parental placement, meaning they didn't go through the Department of Public Health and Human Services but dealt directly with the birth mother.

"So the birth mother could have simply signed away her parental rights to the child and consented to the adoption."

"Not that easy," Frank said. "Under Montana law, she was supposed to have completed three hours of counseling, disclosed the birth family's medical and family history, and reviewed a preplacement evaluation of the adoptive family.

"That's just the first step," he continued. "After the adoption, there is a six-month waiting period where a licensed social worker visits the family and files a report to the judge. At the end of the waiting period, there is a second hearing."

Tommy was nodding to himself. "What you're saying is that there would be a record of the adoption—if it had been legal. What about the birth father?"

"Under law, the birth mother would have to provide information on the location of the other legal parent and any others who were legally entitled to notice of the adoption proceeding. That would include any spouse who the birth parent was married to at the time of conception."

"Unless all of this had been done under the table, so to speak," Tommy said. "So what about a home birth?"

"All you have to do is apply for a birth certificate. It would have been even easier twenty-eight years ago," Edwards said.

"So the so-called adoptive mother could have put anything she wanted on the birth certificate," Tommy said. "She could have passed off the baby as her own. The question is, where did she get the infant?" He checked to see if any infants had been kidnapped about that time in Montana. None.

Where would someone get an infant if they weren't going to steal one? *You buy it*, he thought.

BUCK WASN'T SURPRISED by the grandeur of the house. It was massive, brick, stone and glass, a monument to Harrison Brookshire's success. Multimillion-dollar homes had once been unique in the Bozeman area. Not anymore. Not since a classic three-bedroom house in town now went for almost a million with the influx of people with money looking for a simpler life.

Yet as he walked up the stone front steps, he wondered what it had been like for Ansley growing up here. He couldn't imagine.

It didn't appear that the Brookshires were home. However, there was a five-car garage. He couldn't tell what was parked inside it.

He knocked and waited. A breeze sighed in the nearby pine trees. Beyond them, he could see the tops of the mountains that surrounded the Gallatin Valley. Nearer, he could smell the Gallatin River close by and hear a jet passing over after leaving the busiest airport in Montana just miles away.

The massive wood door was opened by an older woman in a pale blue uniform. She seemed distracted, her attention on whatever was going on behind her. He heard Ansley's raised voice from deep inside the house.

Removing his Stetson, Buck said, "I'm here to see Ansley," and stepped past the distracted woman. She called after him in obvious frustration. He had no idea where he was going—hopefully this was the right direction. He heard the housekeeper close the door, her shoes squeaking as she hurried after him.

He glanced around as he went, finding all the lavish furnishings cold and uninviting. It felt as if someone had staged the house for a potential buyer and none of the furniture had ever been used. A stone fireplace took up almost the entire back wall of the living room. He spotted Ansley off to one side of it. She was going through some cabinets on a nearby wall and had apparently been arguing with the housekeeper.

"Don't tell me you don't know where it is," Ansley was saying as she dug in the cabinet. "Nothing gets moved around here without you knowing about it, Ingrid. Where did my mother put it?"

"Miss," the housekeeper said impatiently as she caught up with Buck. "*Miss!* You have company."

Ansley looked up then, straightening in obvious surprise. *"Buck?"* Those blue eyes widened. "Did you follow me?"

"We should talk about that. In private," he said.

She gave him a look that said, yes, they would be discussing it, before turning again to the housekeeper. "I'm not leaving without that photograph. I'd hate to have to tear this house apart to find it. But I will."

Ingrid sighed heavily. "Perhaps your mother did move it. I'll find out." She seemed to hesitate, as if afraid to leave Ansley alone with the cowboy who'd pushed his way in. With another sigh, she headed for the stairs at a trot.

"She's gone up to tell my adoptive mother on me," Ansley said with a shake of her head. Her gaze settled on him. "You're about to meet Maribelle Brookshire. Brace yourself." She sighed. "How am I going to explain you?"

"What? You've never brought home a cowboy before? I thought it was every woman's dream."

Her laugh was a nervous one, and yet he heard a lightness in it that he liked. Just as he liked her smile. Because of that, he hated to be the one to wipe it away.

"You were followed after you left the motel," he said quietly. "And not just by me. I couldn't see the driver of the pickup, but I did get a plate number. I'll give it to James. Just as I feared, your adoptive parents aren't the only ones who might not want you finding your birth mother."

"Ansley?" A woman's voice floated down the stairs, followed by an elegantly attired blonde woman. "Ingrid says we have company."

"Did she also tell you that I'm looking for that small, framed photo of me when I was five?"

Maribelle Brookshire swept into the room, all smiles. She was a woman who'd done everything money could buy not to look her age. It had worked. "Oh, my," she said when she saw Buck. Smiling, she extended her hand. "I don't believe we've met. I'm—"

"Maribelle Brookshire," he said, taking her limp, cool hand for an instant.

"My reputation must precede me," she said and glanced at Ansley, as if suspecting what he'd heard about her hadn't been nice. Her look, when she returned it to Buck, said, *Don't believe anything my daughter tells you.*

"I just want my photo," Ansley said, crossing her arms over her chest and holding her ground.

"Aren't you going to introduce me to your friend?"

"Buck Crawford," he said. "It's nice to meet you, Mrs. Brookshire." He saw the question in her gaze. She was wondering if he was the PI her daughter had hired and, if so, what he was doing here.

"Mother?"

Maribelle dragged her gaze from him to look at Ansley. "What's this about a photo?"

"You know the one I'm asking about, the one that was on the mantel yesterday when I was here."

The two stared at each other for a full minute before her mother sighed and walked down a short hallway. He heard a door open, then close. When she came back, she handed a small, framed photo to her daughter. Buck could feel the tension between the two.

"I hope you know what you're doing," Maribelle said under her breath before excusing herself. "Is your friend staying for lunch?" she asked before starting back up the grand stairway.

"No, and neither am I," Ansley said, holding the photograph tight to her chest until her mother disappeared from view.

ANSLEY WAS ALMOST afraid to look at the photo. What if she remembered it wrong? What if she looked nothing like the Colt brothers? What if it had all been in her imagination and now she'd dragged the Colts into her delusion? Dragged them into a wishful dream of a family that looked like her?

She held the photo to her chest for a moment longer before she finally looked. Tears rushed to her eyes as she was overwhelmed by emotion. It was just as she remembered. She was one of the Colts. It had to be true. It couldn't be only wishful thinking, and yet the look in her young eyes broke her heart. She remembered that little girl and felt that old pang of loneliness in this big house with only passing glimpses of her parents.

She'd wanted a family, her real family, as far back as she could remember. That desire had been heart deep, as if she'd known all along that she didn't belong here. But had she really found it in the Colts?

Buck took a step toward her, no doubt anxious to see the photo, but he didn't get the chance as the front door slammed open. They both turned as Lanny Jackson stormed in. He was a large man dressed all in black with a face that matched his bad disposition. Ansley clutched the framed photo, determination making her rigid. She had to show this to the Colts, especially James. He had to know that she wasn't delusional. She couldn't wait for the DNA test results. The photo would make him understand why she believed she was one of them.

"I suggest you put that back," Lanny said, dismissing Buck with a brisk wave of his hand as he focused all his ire on her. "I've already alerted your father of an intruder on the estate."

"I'm not an intruder," she snapped. "I have more right to be in this house than you do."

He grunted in answer to that, an ugly grin doing nothing for his face. So far Lanny hadn't acknowledged Buck and continued to ignore him, his gaze on her as he spoke. "As of this afternoon, you aren't allowed to take anything from the house without your father's expressed permission."

She shook her head as if in disbelief. "My mother knows I'm taking the photo. She gave it to me."

Lanny held his ground. "That may well be so, but I work for your father. I can't let you leave with—"

Buck stepped in front of him. "Lanny Jackson, right?

The not-too-smart felon who left his fingerprints at Colt Brothers Investigation yesterday when you ransacked their offices?"

"I don't know who you are or what you're talking about, but this is none of your business," the thug said. "I suggest you leave while you still can."

Ansley could see where this was headed. "Buck, don't—" She didn't want trouble. She especially didn't want this cowboy to get hurt because of her.

"You're really threatening to physically keep Ansley Brookshire from taking her own childhood photo from this house?" Buck asked Lanny, as if he hadn't heard her try to stop him.

Just as she feared, both Buck and Lanny looked ready for a fight.

BUCK HAD KNOWN there would be trouble. Ansley had said she would call her fiancé to come to the house with her. So where was he? And would it have done any good if he'd been here now? He doubted it, unless her fiancé was a cop or an NFL football player or carried a weapon.

He met Lanny Jackson's scowl, saw a twinkle in the man's dark eyes and knew the bodyguard was hoping for a showdown.

"You need to back off." Lanny cocked his head, his hand snaking around to his side. Buck had already noticed the telltale sign that the man was carrying. But just in case he didn't get the hint, the bodyguard brushed his jacket aside and turned just enough so Buck could see the holstered Glock.

Buck smiled and said, "Show me yours and I'll have to show you mine. You sure you want a shoot-out here in this nice house?" He shook his head. "I didn't think so. Ansley, it's time for us to leave." She moved up beside him. He didn't see the framed photo. He figured it was resting next to the one of the Colt brothers in her large purse on her shoulder.

Clearly the bodyguard didn't want to back down. They were about the same height and weight. Buck had grown up wrestling with the wild Colt boys. He knew he could hold his own—unless Lanny Jackson fought dirty. Looking into the man's sneer, Buck knew instinctively that he did.

As he and Ansley stepped forward, Lanny moved to block their way. Buck had to question if this was really about a photograph—or was this man just protecting his turf?

"You need to mind your own business, cowboy," the bodyguard said, getting in his face.

Buck really doubted Lanny would pull his gun—let alone use it here. "You think your employer would appreciate what's about to go down in his living room? How much do you think this rug under our feet costs? Doubt your boss will be able to get the blood out of it. I would hate for any of the fancy furnishings to be destroyed when you and I go at each other. But why don't you call your boss first, because I'm betting whatever we break will come out of *your* wages."

Lanny's jaw tightened. It took a moment or two, but he finally stepped aside to let them leave. "This isn't over."

Buck didn't doubt it. He could tell that it took all the man's self-control to let them go. Lanny wasn't the kind who backed down. Which meant Buck would be seeing the man again. Only next time, it would be an ambush—and there would be blood.

Chapter Nine

"We need to talk," Buck said the moment he and Ansley stepped outside her adoptive parents' house. He watched her turn to look back at the balcony on the second floor. Maribelle Brookshire was standing at the railing, watching them. There was no sign of Lanny Jackson.

"Not here. We can talk at my office in Bozeman," she said. "Do you mind following me? It isn't far."

He thought about the last woman in trouble he'd thought he was saving. Hadn't he learned anything? But after seeing what had transpired at the house earlier, he couldn't walk away now, no matter how dangerous. Maribelle Brookshire had given her daughter the photo that she'd obviously hidden before they'd arrived. Had she really been afraid Ansley would tear the place apart to find it, as she'd threatened the housekeeper? Clearly she hadn't wanted Ansley to take it. Why else would she call Lanny to stop her? What mother would do that? One who had a whole lot to hide, he thought.

On the way into town, Buck called Willie and told him about the pickup following Ansley to the estate.

He gave him the plate number of the vehicle. It took the sheriff only a few minutes before he called back.

"The vehicle matching that description and with those plates belongs to Mark Laden of Mark's Used Cars." Buck knew the fly-by-night business north of Lonesome. "Mark said he saw the pickup missing this morning but just assumed someone had taken it out for a test drive. He was going to check with his wife before reporting it stolen. Apparently, it's a vehicle she loans out occasionally."

"Great, so we have no idea who was driving it."

"Not yet," Willie said. "You followed her to Bozeman? You sure you know what you're getting into?"

Buck laughed. He was in way too deep to stop now, he told himself. "I'll have to get back to you on that." He disconnected as ahead he saw the parking area in front of Ansley Brookshire's jewelry shop and the woman herself waiting for him.

They didn't say a word to each other as they went upstairs to her office. The room was bright and airy, filled with artwork and photographs of interesting jewelry, the windows overlooking busy downtown Bozeman's Main Street. "Your designs?" he asked, intrigued by the jewelry. She nodded. "I haven't seen anything like them before."

That brought a smile. "Thank you."

Buck took the chair she offered him. This woman was talented. She had her life together. At least she had until she'd found out that the Brookshires had lied to her. Now it was as if she'd climbed onto a runaway train. He wanted to pull her off, protect her, because he could feel the heartbreak coming for her.

But one look at the determination in her eyes and he knew he couldn't stop that train any more than he could the one that hit and killed her possible biological father, Del Ransom Colt, ten years ago.

Worse, he'd climbed aboard and was now racing headlong with her—into something that could get him killed this time.

ANSLEY STUDIED THE man sitting across the desk from her. She was still furious over everything that had taken place back at the estate. Buck had taken off his Stetson and now balanced it on his knee. He'd come to her rescue. Again. He was starting to make a habit of it. And worse, she felt herself starting to depend on him.

"I appreciated your help back there at the house, but this was a mistake," she said. Because of her, he'd crossed Lanny and was now in the man's crosshairs. "I've put you in danger. And I'm concerned that you followed me."

Buck chuckled. "Don't worry about me. I can hold my own. When I saw someone following you out of Lonesome, I had to follow them. It's a fatal flaw of mine."

"Like that trust issue you mentioned." She was just starting to realize what she'd done. It was as if she'd thrown a stone into a quiet pool and now the ripples were growing wider and wider, threatening to drown anyone in its path. "I never dreamed that looking for my birth mother would cause this much trouble or get so many people involved."

"You've kicked over an anthill, that's for sure," Buck agreed. "Hard to say who else wants to keep your adoption a secret. But word seems to be out that you're looking for your biological mother. Apparently more than your adoptive parents don't want that to happen."

She listened as he told her what he'd learned from the sheriff after he'd called him with the license plate number and make and model of the vehicle. "The sheriff is looking into it. I didn't get a good look at the driver. Sorry."

"You've already done so much for me." Ansley studied this soft-spoken, good-looking cowboy, remembering how he'd handled Lanny. There was more to him than he let most people see. It seemed almost fateful that their paths had crossed. But should she be worried that he always seemed to be around when she needed him? Or worry that he might not be? "I don't know anything about you."

He grinned, a glint in his eyes. "Not much to know. Raised outside Lonesome, got my butt kicked as kid growing up with the wild Colt brothers, spent my youth helping my dad break horses when we weren't raising rough stock for rodeos." He shrugged. "Decided it wasn't for me after college and joined the state police highway patrol. Left that a while back. Now I'm figuring out what's next. Told you—not much to tell."

"Do you always come to the aid of a woman in trouble?"

His grin faded. "Tell me about you."

"Even less to tell. I grew up believing I was a Brookshire, graduated from college in the arts, followed my dream of designing jewelry. To my surprise, it took off online, so I opened a storefront and had to hire jewelry makers to keep up with the demand." She smiled, hoping she didn't sound as if she were bragging. "It was a dream come true." Her smile faded. "Then I found out that everything I'd thought I knew about myself and my life was a lie."

Her heart ached at the memory of that confusing and yet enlightening moment. "I had no idea wanting to find my birth mother would be met with so much opposition on so many fronts." Ansley shook her head. "I don't understand what's happening or why."

"Neither do I," Buck said, "I'm guessing your fiancé isn't on board?"

She glanced away. "Why would you say that?" When he said nothing, she was forced to look at him.

"Just seems someone tipped Maribelle Brookshire off that you were coming for that photo, giving her just enough time to hide it." He held her gaze. "Hard to know who's trying to stop you. Or who you can trust."

That one hit home, hard. She couldn't trust Maribelle or Harrison. Both had lied to her. Now Gage?

"I know I said I'd call him about going with me to the house for the photo," she said, looking away again. "I did call him, but I changed my mind about asking him to go with me. Truthfully, it seemed silly. I really didn't think there would be a problem."

"Did you happen to tell him what you planned to do?"

She let out a nervous laugh. "You really think my

fiancé warned my mother?" But she could see that's exactly what they both thought.

"Sorry, you know him, and I don't," Buck said. "I guess you were lucky that Maribelle didn't have time to get rid of it."

It was clear that her adoptive mother had been warned, and they both knew it. They also knew who had given her the heads-up—the only person she'd told where she was going and why. Gage had betrayed her. As much as she hated to admit it, she couldn't trust the people closest to her.

Instead, she was now depending on strangers. One stranger in particular, she thought, as she met Buck's gaze again.

BUCK COULD SEE how upset she was, having come to the same conclusion he had. Her fiancé had sold her out. He hoped he got a chance to meet him. He told himself that he wouldn't punch him in the face. Unless the guy asked for it. Ah, hell, he'd punch the man just on general principles.

"After hearing about Lanny Jackson reaching the PI office before you—" he began.

"You think he knew where I was going before I did," she said, nodding. "I only told Maribelle, and I didn't mention Colt Brothers Investigation."

"You'd looked it up online?"

He saw her eyes widen. "How would Lanny— Unless he had access to my phone…" Lanny probably didn't have access, but her fiancé no doubt did. He saw her expression harden as the pieces of the ugly picture began to fall together.

"Someone could have been tracking your internet searches," Buck said. His money was on the fiancé putting the device at least on her phone and probably her computer. "They also could have put other devices on your car." She looked sick as realization settled in. "You sure you want to keep looking for your birth mother? What about your business?"

"My assistant is more than qualified to run things. I've already let her know I won't be in the office for a while. I booked the motel room in Lonesome for a week. I'm not changing my mind. If anything, this only makes me more determined. Whatever everyone is hiding, I plan to expose it, no matter who is involved." She took a breath and let it out slowly as she met his gaze. "But I can't ask you to risk your life for me."

"You're not asking," he said, feeling his chest tighten at her look, his breathing catch. "I've been involved from the moment we collided in the alley. You're actually helping me. In between careers right now, remember. I need the distraction."

She eyed him. "So, I'm a *distraction* and this is just about you amusing yourself between careers?"

He chuckled. "A lovely distraction." No way did he want to believe it was anything but that—as drawn to her as he was. "Seriously? If I can be of help to you and the Colts, all the better."

"James is right. This is more dangerous than I first thought. You met Lanny. I hate to think what could have happened back at the house if you hadn't been there—or worse, if you hadn't talked him down." Her blue eyes shone with worry. "You forced him to back down. He won't forget that. He'll come after you. That was what I was trying to avoid."

He knew there were some much more dangerous ways he could get hurt. "Let me worry about that." He leaned forward, telling himself he'd gotten into this to protect his friends. If she was wrong about her connection to the Colts, then that part would be moot. She'd just be another client. Would he still be so willing to risk his neck for her? He held her gaze. Yep, he'd risk his neck for her, and that should have worried him more than it did. "Mind if I see the photograph you took from the house?"

She reached into her shoulder bag and pulled out the framed snapshot of the Colts, then the one of herself. She put them side by side on her desk, turning them to face him. He could feel her watching his expression as he compared the two.

He studied the photos for a moment, then looked up at her. She'd already seen the same thing that he now had. She was the spitting image of the Colt brothers at that age.

She nodded. "You see why I can't stop now. I have to know."

HARRISON BROOKSHIRE PACED the floor of his office, his cell phone held away from his ear as Maribelle yelled obscenities at him.

"Some bodyguard you hired," she snapped. "He let

her and that cowboy just walk out of the house with the photo."

"What photo?" he asked, trying to understand what had happened, and, more important, what any of this had to do with him. She knew better than to bother him at work.

"The photo Gage called me about. He warned me that she was coming to get it. You know, the one taken when she was… I don't know what age, little, just a kid. She wanted it, because she thought it proved who she was. At least that's what Gage said. She plans to show it to the private investigator she hired in Lonesome."

Harrison couldn't believe what he was hearing. "What in hell's name have you gotten us into, Maribelle?" he demanded. "I never wanted a child. I told you that. But you just had to have a daughter, and like everything you've just had to have, you lost interest right away. And now she's turned on us."

"Not this again. I don't need another lecture from you," she snapped. "What are you planning to do about her?"

"What would you have me do?" he yelled back. He could feel his blood pressure rising to a dangerous level. If only he had stopped her all those years ago. Had he really thought that a daughter would make his wife happy and keep her out of his hair?

"I don't care what you do as long as you stop her before she ruins us. Our daughter has lost her mind. I seriously think she needs help—maybe to be admitted to an institution until she comes to her senses. Now she's hooked up with some cowboy who even your so-called bodyguard was too afraid to stop."

He groaned inwardly. "What cowboy?"

"I think he said his name was Buck Crawford."

"Is he the private investigator?"

"I don't think so. I have no idea where she picked him up. Gage was beside himself when I called and told him about it after she left with that man. Dear, sweet Gage— he said he's done his best to dissuade her from this foolish quest of hers, but not even her fiancé seems to be able to reason with her. He agrees with me that if Ansley doesn't change her mind, something awful might happen to her. I don't think he'll break off the engagement. But I can't bear the thought of that bit of information hitting the news, not to mention social media—"

"Embarrassing you is the least of my worries," Harrison snapped. "I thought you handled this with the money I gave you."

"I'm working on that end, but unless Gage can stop Ansley—"

"Maribelle," Harrison said, talking over her. As if things weren't bad enough, she seemed determined to stir the pot by bringing Gage into whatever this was. "Don't wind Gage up. She's lucky to have a man like him. Let me handle this. You go on about your business and leave it to me."

He disconnected and walked to his office bar. He poured himself a shot and downed it, afraid of what Maribelle had done. At this point, he just had to deal with it, and as quickly as possible, from the sounds of it. He hadn't gotten to where he was in life by backing down when things got tough. He wouldn't this time. Yet although he knew there was only one way to handle this, he hesitated. He'd learned in business that sometimes it took a drastic move to get the outcome he wanted.

Pulling out his phone, he made the call. "This has to be handled very carefully and even more quickly and quietly." He disconnected and poured himself another shot. Downing it, he told himself there was no other way. He certainly couldn't afford to grow a conscience at this point in his life.

Chapter Ten

James couldn't help being frustrated with this case. Finding Ansley's birth mother was proving to be like looking for a needle in a haystack. Tommy had researched everything he could find out about adoption in Montana. Even if the adoption had been legal and aboveboard, under the law, the birth mother could keep her offspring from contacting her or learning her name.

If this was a back-porch adoption like he suspected, then even if money had changed hands, it would be hard to prove. They might never know the truth.

Ansley hadn't been adopted legally. That much they knew. Where to go from here— He felt discouraged as his cell phone rang.

"Hey," he said, seeing that it was his wife. He waited for the sound of Lori's voice, needing to hear it right now.

When she finally spoke, there was an edge to it that he knew too well. "I want to meet her," she said, getting right to it. "Invite her to dinner."

James cursed his baby brother, Davy. Newly married, Davy had confided to his bride, Carla, about Ansley Brookshire. Davy knew better than to talk about their cases, but James was sure this had hit too close to home to for Davy keep it from Carla and for Carla to keep it from Lori.

"I don't talk about cases, you know that," James said. "And I sure as the devil don't invite clients to dinner."

She made a dismissive sound. "This woman might be your sister and you don't think we should meet her?"

"Half sister, but we don't know that for a fact and won't until the DNA test results come back, so I don't see any reason to—"

"Well, I do. I want to meet her," Lori said definitively. "I heard she's staying at the motel, paid for a whole week. Even if she isn't your sister, she thinks she is, and that's good enough for me. Family is family. Invite her to dinner. In fact, I want the whole family here." He started to argue, but she cut him off. "I've talked to the wives, and we all agree. Our house tonight."

"What is the rush? We could have the DNA results any day—"

"Please?" He could almost see her giving him that look he knew so well. It was a look he couldn't resist— even just imagining it over the phone. "Please, James. If there is any chance she's your sister… Don't disappoint me."

"Never," he said and had to smile as she disconnected. He knew how his wife felt about family. Add that to the pregnancy, and you didn't argue with a woman running on hormones. He could have called her back and argued his case, literally, but he was too smart for that. Also, she was right. If there was a chance that Ansley might be family… He still didn't want to believe his father had kept something like this from them. If Del Ransom Colt had, then they hadn't known him at all. James wasn't ready to go there.

He picked up the phone. "Do you have plans for dinner tonight?" he asked, clearly catching Ansley off guard. "I know it's short notice. The whole family will be there. Buck's coming." He hadn't yet asked him, but that didn't stop James. He still had hopes that his friend would be joining the agency. "I'm sure he'll give you a ride out to the ranch. Seems everyone wants to meet you."

After he hung up, he called Buck's number, not surprised to learn he was with Ansley in Bozeman. Buck told him what had been going on. He listened, shaking his head. Someone had borrowed an old pickup from Mark's used car lot and followed Ansley to the Brookshire Estate.

"She got the photo," Buck was saying. "Lanny Jackson tried to stop her. I'm pretty sure I'll be seeing him again."

"Buck." The news didn't get better. "Her fiancé ratted her out to Maribelle Brookshire?"

"Looking forward to meeting the fiancé one day," Buck said. "I'm willing to bet he's responsible for the tracking devices on Ansley's car, phone and computer as well as inside her condo. I removed all of them I could find. I told her to hire someone to sweep her office as well."

James groaned. "You realize what you're saying, don't

you? The people around her are determined to stop her. Stop you. Stop us from finding out the truth."

"And she's just as determined to keep going. I'm going to follow her back to Lonesome. She's taken a room at the motel for a week," Buck said. "She got the photo from the estate. You're going to want to see it, James. If she isn't related to you, I'll eat one of my lucky boots."

"The leather on your lucky boots is thin enough. With some steak sauce, you'll probably enjoy it. Seriously, Buck, be careful. Also, I don't know if Ansley mentioned it or not, but Lori is having the whole family over tonight for dinner at our place at seven. I told Ansley you'd bring her. After dinner, I was hoping we could talk."

"Sure. But James, the Brookshires are serious about not wanting her to find her birth mother. I'm afraid of what they'll do next."

"I'm afraid of what you'll do next," James said but realized his friend had already disconnected.

JUDY RAMSEY HAD never expected to hear from Maribelle Brookshire ever again. She told herself that she would have been fine with that. For years she'd tried to put what they did behind her. Nasty business, her mother would have said. She'd felt dirty, as if she had blood on her hands, giving a woman like Maribelle Brookshire a baby.

She never would have done it except that almost thirty years ago, she'd been desperate. Not that that was a good excuse. It was just the truth. Had she been able to do it again, she would have never let Maribelle talk her into it.

So why was the woman calling her now? Judy considered her current situation and tried to assure herself that it could be good news. Maribelle would want something from her, that was a given. But there would also be a reward, and let's face it, the years hadn't been that good, Judy had to admit. She was getting too old to wait tables. Her legs had been bothering her. Her back, too.

How much money could she get out of the woman this time, though? Would it be worth it to meet her? With a shudder, she reminded herself who she was dealing with. Maribelle wasn't like normal people. She made up her own rules. That's what too much money and power did to a person.

As Judy sat on the back steps of her house smoking, she kept wondering why the woman wanted to see her now, after all these years. It couldn't bode well, could it?

For a moment, she thought about not going to the meeting. But she knew that wouldn't stop the woman. She felt torn, but she needed to know what this was about. Best to find out what she wanted. And if there was money involved, well, she'd take it.

She felt a chill as she crushed out her cigarette. The last thing she wanted was to get involved with this woman again. The last time, she hadn't felt as if she had an option. Did she really this time, either? Judy had kept their secret for more than twenty-eight years. She lit another cigarette. Whatever Maribelle wanted, she'd better bring a lot of money tonight, because this was going to cost her.

JAMES WAS JUST about to call it a day and go home and help Lori get ready for the dinner tonight when Ansley Brookshire walked into the PI office. He hadn't expected to see her until later at the ranch.

She headed right for his desk without preamble. She pulled a small, framed photo from her shoulder bag and laid it down in front of him. She then pulled out the framed photo that had graced the Colt office wall for as long as James could remember and set it next to the first.

With the photos side by side, he looked down, first taking in the one of him and his brothers. He really would have been heartbroken if he hadn't gotten the photo back, because he had no idea what had happened to the original or the negative. The photo had been taken before digital snapshots on cell phones.

His gaze shifted to the girl in the other photo. He felt his heart do a whoop-de-do in his chest, stealing his breath, before he looked up at her.

"Yeah," he said. That was the best he could do. He felt as if he'd been punched. "I'm told we should have the preliminary DNA test results soon. Then…there won't be any doubt." Not that there was much doubt now, he thought as he met her blue eyes. So familiar, just as Buck had said.

Meanwhile, he had to tell Ansley that so far he hadn't learned much on her case and neither had Tommy. By whatever means Maribelle Brookshire had gotten baby Ansley, she'd done a good job of covering her tracks.

James explained what the agency had been doing since they'd last talked. She listened, appearing not surprised. Davy was still tied up in a case down in Wyoming, so it was just James and Tommy doing the legwork. "Tommy is following the money trail, seeing who came into unexplained money about twenty-eight years ago. He's also checking on births in town and nearby and trying to find midwives from that time, since we don't believe you were born in the hospital. Twenty-eight years ago in Montana, the birth mother would have been required to fill out the birth certificate before leaving the hospital. So there would have been a record. Except there's none."

ANSLEY WASN'T SURPRISED. She'd done enough research to know that Maribelle hadn't gone through proper channels. The only thing that had surprised her had been the dinner invitation. The family wanted to meet her? The thought scared her and, at the same time, filled her with hope. They were taking this seriously.

"My searches have reached the same conclusion," she told James. "What can I do to help?" The thought of just hanging around every day waiting was killing her. She wanted this over with, and as quickly as possible. "Please. I've taken a room at the motel in town, and I'm staying as long as it takes. Tell me what I can do."

James glanced up as Buck came into the office. "You could talk to anyone who worked for the family at the time you were brought home as an infant. Gardeners, housekeepers—anyone who knew that your adoptive mother wasn't pregnant before you arrived at the house. They might have some idea where she got the baby, especially if she had to leave for any length of time to pick you up."

She nodded. She'd talked to her first nanny but hadn't thought about the other staff. She knew how household staff liked to gossip. Also given how many Maribelle had fired over the years, she thought some might be more honest with her and less afraid to talk.

"I also plan to visit the yarn shop," she said. "I know it's a long shot that someone there might remember a woman who bought yarn nearly thirty years ago, but I have to try."

James agreed. "Toni might be more apt to talk to you than me."

"I'll go with her," Buck said.

Ansley saw a look pass between James and Buck. "I just want to be sure that she's safe," Buck said. "So, if it's all right with Ansley…"

"I'm hoping Buck will be joining the investigation," James said. "With his background in law enforcement, we could really use him—at least on this case." Another look passed between them. One she couldn't read.

She smiled at Buck, who'd been standing by the door, already proving that he planned to keep an eye on her. She told them about what she knew regarding the pink baby blanket believed to have been made by her birth mother.

"Why would she buy both blue and pink?" James asked. "Wouldn't you find out the gender if you were going to all the trouble of knitting a baby blanket?"

Ansley had to smile as she imagined her birth mother making two blankets because she didn't want to know before her baby was born. "Maybe she didn't want to know because she couldn't keep me." She looked to Buck, to see if he understood, and got a nod.

"She would have gotten more attached otherwise," he said. "I get it. So she was ready with both blankets when the baby was born."

Except Ansley couldn't imagine how hard it must have been for her birth mother to go home empty-handed with only the blue blanket that she'd knit.

JUDY WASN'T LOOKING forward to a clandestine meeting with Maribelle Brookshire, but she was curious. Something must have happened to shake the woman. Why else were they meeting? That thought brought a smile.

She was feeling better by the time she pulled onto the old river highway. She dodged potholes and tried to convince herself that meeting Mrs. High and Mighty was a good thing. The woman must need her help again.

Judy told herself that she could put up with Maribelle looking down her nose at her just fine—as long as it paid well. It had the last time. This time, she'd demand more—after all, she knew Maribelle Brookshire's darkest secrets, didn't she?

It wasn't like she'd treated the woman as if she was a bottomless well that she could tap whenever she needed a decent drink. She'd kept her mouth shut and never asked for more money. But to have Maribelle call her asking to see her? This was one of those times when the sky could be the limit. The woman had sounded desperate, which made Judy wonder why. What if the cops had gotten wind of what they'd done? Maybe Maribelle was looking for a fall guy and this was a setup? The woman could even be wearing a wire.

No, Judy decided. The last thing Maribelle wanted was the cops involved. With her money, she could keep that from happening. It was something personal, something about the girl. Judy realized that the baby she'd given Maribelle was a young woman by now. Had it really been that many years?

Maybe it was time to make a major withdrawal from that well—just in case there was any chance of it going completely dry.

Pulling off the old river highway to the spot where Maribelle had said to meet, she stopped short. The old motel and restaurant looked abandoned. She spotted a for-sale sign propped up in front of the dirty front window of the café. How long had it been closed? Probably since the new highway had passed it by.

What she hadn't expected was for the area to be so isolated. A car hadn't passed since she'd turned off onto the decaying asphalt. She felt a shiver of trepidation. The entire place was miles from anything, in the middle of Montana, on a road that clearly didn't get much traffic anymore.

For a moment, she thought about hightailing it out of there before Maribelle arrived. She could call her, suggest somewhere a little less spooky to meet. But at the sound of a car pulling in next to hers, she realized it was too late. Maribelle had arrived. Best to just get this over with, since Judy definitely could use the money. If she put it off, Maribelle might change her mind.

As she looked over at the fancy car and the person

sitting behind the wheel, she was surprised the woman had come alone. She'd expected to see some huge bodyguard. She'd just assumed Maribelle would bring one with her. She had brought backup the last time they'd met at some off the beaten path. But that had been almost thirty years ago. Maybe Maribelle Brookshire trusted her this time.

Judy pushed aside her earlier trepidation. The woman wouldn't have called her unless she needed her help. Still, she waited. *Let her come to me.* The driver's side door of the expensive car opened, and Maribelle stepped out wearing a suit and high heels. Maybe that's all she owned, but she looked ridiculous all dressed up like that out here. She'd mostly seen Maribelle's photo at some social event in the newspaper or society magazines. Judy had made the newspaper only once—for a DUI when she was younger.

Maribelle flung a large designer purse over one shoulder as if she was on her way to a board meeting. If she hoped to intimidate her, the woman didn't know her very well.

Maribelle didn't know her at all. Their brief acquaintance had been more of a business arrangement. Money exchanged hands and so did a baby, Judy reminded herself—as if she could ever forget.

The first time she'd laid eyes on Maribelle had been on the Brookshire Estate, as it was known. Judy had been visiting a friend in Bozeman. "This wealthy woman is throwing a party," her friend had said. "The caterer needs more servers. The money is really good. I'm working it. I could put in a good word if you're interested."

Judy hadn't wanted to be impressed when she'd seen the place, but she was blown away by the opulence. She couldn't imagine having that kind of money, let alone throwing a party like that one. The pay had been really good, and there was plenty of leftover food and champagne. She had indulged as she helped clean up the kitchen, even though she knew she shouldn't.

And later, throwing up in the guest bathroom, that's when she'd met Maribelle Brookshire. She'd expected a tongue-lashing. Instead, the woman had been sympathetic. She'd handed her a warm, wet washcloth as Judy had apologized.

"Pregnant?" Maribelle had asked.

She remembered blinking in surprise. It wasn't like she was showing. She'd only suspected the previous week. It was why she was in Bozeman. She was hoping her friend would tell her what to do, since the father didn't even know. Wouldn't have made a difference, anyway. He wasn't available. She was on her own.

That night, all those years ago, the woman still dressed in her fancy party clothes had sat down on a teak bench she'd pulled from the shower and told Judy how desperately she wanted a baby. No, not a baby—a daughter. "Is it a girl?"

Judy had said yes, hoping it was true, because she'd seen the gleam in the woman's eyes and realized what this could mean for her. The answer to all her problems. And if she was having a boy? Well, the woman would just have to be glad to get a baby of any gender.

Now, all these years later, Maribelle didn't even glance in her direction before walking over to a worn wooden shelter over a weathered picnic table, its green paint peeling off in clumps. Apparently the woman just assumed she was going to follow her, Judy thought, still sitting behind the wheel of her car.

For a moment, she considering starting the engine and driving away, imaging Maribelle's shocked expression. She shoved away the impulse and got out to follow her. *This had better be worth it.*

Chapter Eleven

The shop where her birth mother had purchased both pink and blue yarn also sold baby clothes, some maternity wear, and a few bolts of fabric. As in most small Montana towns, businesses had to diversify to keep the doors open. The shop itself was located inside a larger building that had been divided into smaller commercial spaces.

The sign in the window read simply Toni's. That was another thing Ansley had noticed about small Montana towns—signage was often sparse if it existed at all. If you lived in Lonesome, you knew what Toni's sold. If you didn't, well, then, you probably weren't going to shop there.

When she commented on this to Buck as they entered the shop, he laughed and said, "For some old-timers, their attitude is that if you don't know where you're going, then you have no business here."

Toni turned out to be a tiny woman with short gray hair and a huge welcoming smile. Buck had told Ansley that Toni had started the shop years ago, so there was the chance that she'd known the woman who'd bought the yarn.

They both knew it was a long shot, though, that she would remember a purchase all those years ago.

"Buck Crawford, I declare. I don't think I've ever seen you in my shop." Toni grinned as she shifted her gaze to Ansley. "What brings you in today?"

"Actually, I have a strange request," Ansley said. "I'm looking for a pregnant woman who bought yarn from you in the spring almost thirty years ago."

Toni's eyes widened. Ansley rushed on. "The woman bought both pink and blue, as if she wasn't sure what she was having."

"Honey, I barely can remember what I had for breakfast. Why would you be looking for someone who bought yarn all those years ago?"

"I believe she was my birth mother. I'm trying to find her."

Toni seemed at a loss for words. She looked at Buck, then back to Ansley. "Oh, honey, I wish I could help. Even if I kept records of all purchases, I wouldn't have any that far back anymore."

Ansley couldn't help feeling crestfallen. She knew it had been an incredible long shot, and yet she'd still gotten her hopes up. "Thanks, I understand. I just thought you would have…remembered her. A beginning knitter. Maybe she asked for help." She could see that nothing she could say was going to trigger a memory. "Thank you for your time, anyway."

"Wait," Toni said as Ansley started to turn away. "I remember a lot of my customers. Pink and blue yarn. What did she make?"

"A baby blanket. My nanny told me it was quite a

simple pattern. That's why she thought my mother was just learning to knit."

Toni raised an eyebrow at the word *nanny* but said, "Leave me your phone number. There aren't that many knitters in town, although this sounds like it might have been a onetime purchase. If I think of someone who could help you, I'll give you a call."

Ansley thanked her and left her number.

"Sorry," Buck said as they walked out.

"I knew it was a long shot. But for a moment there…" Ansley thought she'd seen a flash of recognition, as if the shop owner had remembered something.

Once outside, she glanced back and saw Toni talking on the phone. She looked excited and turned her back as if keeping her voice down.

Ansley knew the call might have nothing to do with her, but she didn't believe it. Had Toni called her birth mother to warn her?

If so, her mother didn't want to be found. She couldn't help feeling defeated. With so many people trying to keep her from it, did she even stand a chance of ever learning the truth?

WILLIE HAD THE day off. He'd spent his morning calling engraving shops in the area around Lonesome. Each call took time, as most businesses almost thirty years ago hadn't gone to computers. He'd waited while an employee dug through the files. No engraving with the name DelRae with that spelling.

He was about to widen his search area when a young female employee came back on the line.

"I found it." She sounded triumphant. "DelRae." She spelled it out. "That it?"

His pulse pounded. "That's it. Was the necklace purchase there at your store?"

"It was. Looks like the engraving was free."

"Who purchased it?" He held his breath.

For a moment, there was no answer. "Sorry, looks like the person paid cash."

No, he couldn't get this close and then find out nothing. "But didn't they have to wait for the engraving? Didn't they leave a telephone number or a name?"

"Looks like they said they'd come back to get it."

He groaned silently. "So we have no way of knowing if it was a woman or a man." He had another thought. "Did the person have to fill anything out?"

She seemed to brighten. "They had to put down the name they wanted engraved on the piece and sign the form. You can't believe the people who come back and say, 'That isn't the engraving I wanted.' This way we have proof."

"Good for you," he said, meaning it. "Can you read the name?"

"Sorry. It's pretty sloppy and faded."

"That's okay. Can you take a photo of whatever is written on the form and send it to me?" He would recognize his father's handwriting anywhere. He gave her the information and thanked her while he waited for the text.

ANTSY, WORRIED ABOUT this dinner with the Colt family and with no desire to go back to her motel room, Ansley told Buck that she was going back to the PI office.

"James suggested I try to contact former Brookshire employees who might remember something about the time I was born," she told him. "I need to keep busy."

He nodded as he understood. "I want to help, too. Tell me what I can do."

While Ansley tracked down former Brookshire employees from the time Maribelle brought her to the estate, Buck checked to find out if any babies had been stolen during that same time period in the state and the surrounding states.

They took separate offices at Colt Brothers Investigation, promising to holler if they found something. Ansley tracked down the gardener who'd worked for the Brookshires about the time Maribelle brought her home. Les Owens had sounded surprised by her call.

"Why would you be asking questions about that?" he asked in a grating, impatient older voice.

"Because I'm that baby now grown. You were working there when Maribelle brought me home?" A grunt. "Do you remember seeing my mother pregnant with me?"

"What kind of question is that?" he snapped.

She decided to be as direct as he was being. "I know she didn't give birth to me. Do you know where she got me?"

Silence, then, "Maybe a stork brought you to her."

Ansley sighed. "I really could use your help."

"Maybe she found you somewhere."

"Stole me, you mean?" she asked, heart in her throat.

"Or got a good deal on you."

She tried to form the next sentence carefully. "From whom?"

More silence. For a moment, she thought he'd hung up. "Where are you looking?" he asked, almost whispering.

"Lonesome, Montana." She heard the office door open a crack and saw Buck. "Is that where she got me?" She glanced at Buck and saw that, like her, he was waiting for the answer.

"I'd be real careful if I was you about crossing the Brookshires. If you really are the daughter, you should already know that." With that he disconnected. She put down the phone and told Buck about their conversation. "He suggested that she bought me. When I mentioned Lonesome, he told me to be careful."

Buck shook his head. "No record of any infant being kidnapped or taken during that time. I checked for both years since we don't know exactly when you were born, necessarily. Nothing. Sorry."

"He could have just been toying with me," she said with a sigh.

"How about lunch?" he suggested. "There's a diner down the street."

Her cell phone rang. She didn't recognize the number. For just an instant, she thought it might be Les Owens calling back from a different phone. Maybe he hadn't been able to talk freely earlier. But it was a female voice. It took a moment for her to recognize it. "Toni?"

"Can you stop back by the shop? I think I might know who you're looking for."

"We'll be right there," she said.

TONI WAS WAITING for them when Buck and Ansley reached the shop. She motioned them back into her office, closing the door behind them and clearing away boxes of yarn that hadn't been unpacked to make room for them to sit on two plastic chairs she dragged up.

Ansley noted that the woman seemed nervous. "You thought of someone who might have purchased the yarn?" It seemed such a long shot, she still didn't believe it possible. But that didn't keep her from hoping.

"I wouldn't even have remembered someone buying yarn so many years go except for the pink and blue— and you mentioning that you thought she might be new to knitting," Toni said and took a breath before continuing. "It rang a bell. I called the woman who used to work for me part-time. We had laughed that day because of who came in to buy the yarn, a how-to-knit book and knitting needles. But that's not why we remembered. She was the last person on earth we thought would take up knitting, let alone buy a pattern for a baby blanket."

Before Ansley could ask why that was the case, Buck spoke up. "Someone local, then?"

Toni looked at him and whispered, "Judy Ramsey."

Ansley looked from Toni to Buck and back. "Why would that be so strange? Who is Judy Ramsey?"

"There are just some people you don't expect to take up knitting," Buck said, as if to remind Toni that they might be talking about Ansley's birth mother.

"We had no idea she was pregnant," Toni said. "We just never thought she'd actually knit a blanket, but you said she did—if it's the same woman. Who knew?

Just didn't seem the type. She'd never been in the shop before—or after."

"But you saw her that day when she bought the yarn, and she was pregnant?" Ansley asked.

"She wasn't showing, if that's what you're asking," the shop owner said. "We didn't see her again, because she didn't return to the shop. We were trying to remember, but we think she was working in an old folks' home down in Lincoln. When she came back to Lonesome to go to work at the café, she didn't look pregnant, and she didn't have a baby."

"So it could be her?" Ansley asked hopefully, her voice cracking as she looked over at Buck. "Do you know where we can find her?"

"I do," Buck said. They thanked Toni and left the shop.

"What is it about Judy Ramsey that you were trying to get Toni not to say?" she demanded once they were outside and alone on the street.

He seemed to hesitate. "She had a hard life. Made some poor choices when it came to men, I think. As far as I knew, she never had any kids. Twenty-eight years ago she would have been in her late thirties, early forties. Her being pregnant would have been a surprise, that's all."

It wasn't all. She waited giving him a look that finally made him speak.

"It's just that Judy had kind of a reputation around town. She tended to be attracted to other women's husbands," he said.

"And she might be my mother." It wasn't a question.

"Buck, I had no expectations when I started this." That was mostly true. "I know I might not like what I find. I just have to know. I can't let this go until I do. Where can I find her?"

"I'll take you. She lives close by. We can walk if you want."

It was a short walk. They left the business district behind and walked into the older residential area. As they did, the houses got smaller and so did the yards. Before long they were in an area where most of the houses needed paint and repairs. The yards were filled with junk or the parts of vehicles, kids' bikes or rusting motorcycles.

Judy Ramsey lived in a small house with several cluttered vacant lots between her and her neighbor.

"Her car isn't here," Buck said—nor was the pickup that had followed Ansley to the Brookshire Estate, he added.

Still, Ansley went up to the door and knocked. Someone had put plants out at the edge of the porch but appeared to have forgotten to water them. She peered in through a crack in the curtained window of the door. It was neat enough inside, but she caught the smell of old cigarette smoke and saw an overflowing ashtray next to one of the porch plants.

Was this the woman who'd given her life and then given her up? She kept thinking about the knit blanket. She'd cared. Ansley held on to that like a life raft in the rough sea of her emotions.

As they were heading back to the office, Buck took a call. "You're sure about that? Okay." He disconnected and looked over at her. "Sounds like someone from the mayor's office borrowed that pickup that followed you to the Brookshire Estate." He glanced at the time. "Too late to stop by today. In fact, we'd better get ready for dinner." He smiled and added, "It's going to be fun—you'll see."

Fun? She doubted that, as she tried to ignore the butterflies already flitting around her stomach. She would feel like she was on trial. They would be trying to decide if she was one of them.

MARIBELLE WAITED, her irritation growing. Why didn't the woman get out of her car? What was she waiting for? She was furious that it had come to this. She'd sworn she would never see the woman again—as long as Judy Ramsey kept her mouth shut.

But with Ansley determined to open this can of worms, she'd been left little choice. She just hoped to remind Judy to keep her mouth shut now more than ever.

But first she needed to find out if the foolish woman had ever told anyone—and if there was anything the PIs could find that would lead them to her.

At the sound of a car door opening and closing, Maribelle pulled herself together. She didn't want to come off as desperate—even though she was. Judy would smell fear and try to rob her blind.

In the mood Maribelle was in, that would be bad for Judy's health.

She hugged her large, expensive leather purse, feeling the weight of the gun inside. She'd promised herself that she wouldn't use it. She would just pay the woman

off like last time. She'd make it clear there wouldn't
be any more money in the future—once she was sure
that the woman had kept her mouth shut all these years.

As Judy Ramsey walked toward her, she noticed she
was limping a little. The woman had aged, and not in a
good way, Maribelle thought. Maybe she was the desperate one. It gave her hope that this could be handled
without any bloodshed.

THE SPRING SKY had filled with clouds that obscured the
sun and darkened the pines all around the old motel
and café not far from Lonesome. Squalls were building along the horizon. They'd be lucky if they didn't get
caught in another snowstorm, she thought.

"What's this about?" Judy asked with a sigh, hoping to rush along whatever it was as she faced Maribelle. The woman had had work done. She didn't look
all that much older than the last time she'd seen her.
"I need to get to my job. Some of us have to work." It
was a lie. She had taken some time off after injuring
her leg on the job.

"I'll make this brief," Maribelle said from her high
horse. "My daughter found out that she was adopted."

Judy felt her eyebrows arch up. *"You never told her?"*
Maribelle gave her an impatient look. "You didn't tell
her because you never wanted her to know that someone
else carried her for nine months, through morning sickness and weight gain, before spending hours pushing
her out of her womb and going through all that pain."

"Before giving her away without a second thought
for money?" Maribelle snapped. "No, I didn't. Maybe I

should have told her that her mother didn't want her—
sold her for fifty thousand dollars." She made it sound
like that wasn't even that much money.

Judy saw contempt in those eyes and felt anger burn
in hers. She'd provided this woman with the daughter
she just had to have. The woman had no idea how hard
that had been or what she'd had to go through to pull
it off. Maribelle should be grateful to her. "What is it
you want from me now?"

Maribelle recoiled. "I don't want *anything*. I just
never want my daughter to know about you."

Judy couldn't help being insulted. "Let's not start
throwing stones, okay? I have a few I could fling back
at you. Just spit it out. What did you get me out here
for if you don't want anything? You want *something*.
It's just a matter of how much you're willing to pay for
my silence this time."

Maribelle's blue eyes darkened, her body going still.
Judy realized that she'd overstepped, but she didn't care.
This woman couldn't treat her like this. Judy was the
one with all the knowledge—thus all the power here.

Maribelle took her time answering. "My daughter
has been asking questions about her birth mother," she
said without looking at her. "She's determined to find
her."

Judy couldn't hide her surprise. The girl had grown
up in the lap of luxury. Why would she care about the
mother who'd given her away?

A meadowlark sang close by. The breeze whispered
in the new green leaves of the nearby aspen trees. In

the distance, she thought she could hear the hum of vehicles on Interstate 90.

"I need to know how many people knew about your pregnancy." Maribelle's voice sounded calm—maybe too calm.

"I told you, no one. I went to the place in the mountains I told you about. Everything went as you planned. I called you when the baby was born, we agreed on a spot to meet and you picked her up. We never saw each other again. That was it." She didn't know how Maribelle had gotten the baby a birth certificate. She should have assumed the woman had passed the baby off as her own. She hadn't cared. The money had been badly needed, Maribelle had taken care of all her expenses for those months, and she hadn't had to deal with the woman ever again. Things had worked out satisfactorily for them both.

"Look, I told you I'd keep my mouth shut, and I have. So what if your daughter wants to find her birth mother? She won't. If somehow she finds me, I'd deny it." She shrugged. "You have nothing to worry about."

"I wish that were true. I need to know if there is anything, anything at all, that she could find."

Judy frowned. "Like what?"

"Did you tell anyone, leave a trail, anything that can come back on me?"

She raised a brow, noticing the way Maribelle clutched the large leather purse hanging from her shoulder. "We had a deal. I promised you I wouldn't."

Maribelle scoffed at that. "Promises are often broken."

That was true enough, but Judy was still insulted. "I

don't break *my* promises." Didn't Maribelle realize that Judy would never want any of this coming out, either? "Something else is going on here. What is it?"

The woman took her time answering, clearly not wanting to tell her. "My daughter has hired Colt Brothers Investigation to find her birth mother."

Judy felt gutted. She knew the Colt brothers. They'd already proven they would turn over every rock to solve other cases, including one cold case.

"You promised that no one would ever know," Judy said between clenched teeth.

"And I've tried to keep my promise. Don't you think I've done everything I could to stop Ansley? She is a stubborn young woman, mule headed and unyielding." Maribelle glared at her as if putting the blame on her. "So I ask you again, is there anything these PIs will find that will lead them to you—and ultimately to me?"

"Ansley?" Her name was Ansley? "I thought you promised to name her after her father like I asked?"

Maribelle waved a hand impatiently through the air. "Just answer the question. I don't have all day."

Judy felt sick to her stomach. Promises get broken? So it seemed. She was suddenly fueled with anger. This horrible woman. Why had she ever given her that precious baby? Guilt knifed into her heart. Money. Desperation. Greed. She swallowed down the bile that rose in her throat.

"I don't feel like I can trust you," she said, feeling as if she'd sold her soul to the devil.

Maribelle looked shocked. "Trust *me*?"

Furious and scared, she told herself she didn't want

anything from this woman. If money changed hands, the Colt brothers would find out once she started spending it and come looking for her. One of the wives used to be a loan officer at the bank. They might already be looking for her, checking up on where she got the money to buy her house—money she'd said she inherited back then.

"Why should I tell you anything?" Judy demanded. "Our...arrangement is over. You didn't keep your promise—why should I?" She started to turn away. "Maybe I'll save the Colt brothers the bother of trying to find me and tell them what they want to know."

"I brought money."

She stopped and closed her eyes, her back to Maribelle. *Magic words*, she thought with so much pain that it almost doubled her over. Her life hadn't gone anything like she'd planned. Karma? Payback for what she'd done?

She'd sold her soul once. Was she really going to do it again?

Judy turned slowly, avoiding even looking at the woman. With enough money she could leave town and not look back. "How much money?" When Maribelle didn't answer, she finally faced her.

The gun surprised Judy. She hadn't been expecting it, but the experienced way Maribelle handled it surprised her even more. Judy looked from the weapon to the woman holding it. "You don't want to do that. I took out some insurance in case you ever—" But that's all she got out before she felt the hard slam of the bullet hit her chest. The shock of it made her tumble backward off the picnic table bench. As she fell, she grabbed for the edge of the table and felt a sliver slice into her hand. Her head hit the cracked concrete slab hard; lights flashed before her eyes as she fought to breathe.

As if the words she'd spoken had just now registered, Maribelle moved to stare down at her. "Insurance? What are you talking about?"

Judy tried to smile, not sure if her lips were moving or not. A strange coldness was seeping into her. Her words came out slurred as darkness intruded into her vision. "You're screwed." She didn't even feel the second shot or any of the others as Maribelle kept firing, screaming in frustration and fury, as she emptied the weapon into Judy's lifeless body.

Chapter Twelve

Ansley thought she'd feel like a bug under a microscope at James and Lori's dinner that night. While she was anxious to meet the rest of the family, she couldn't help being nervous about the invitation. She figured the wives were curious. She was curious about them as well, but she was also distracted even before Buck picked her up at the motel.

Before they'd headed out of town toward Colt Ranch, Buck had, at her request, swung by Judy Ramsey's place again. Still nobody home. Ansley feared the woman had heard she was looking for her and taken off. At lunch at the diner where she worked, they were told that she'd taken a few days off.

"You'll like them," Buck said as if reading her mind as he drove out toward the Colt Ranch. "They're nice people."

"James doesn't want to believe that I'm his sister. Even his half sister."

"He doesn't want to believe that his father had a child with a woman they'd never met, and he kept it a secret from them," Buck said.

"Even if I'm their half sister, I still have no idea who my birth mother is."

"That's why you hired the Colt brothers." He glanced over at her. "They're good. If anyone can find her, it's them."

"Maybe we already have found her and that's why she isn't around," Ansley said.

"Let's not go there until we know for sure. By the way, you look beautiful."

His last words made her glance over at him in surprise.

He grinned. "I wanted to say something when I picked you up. Didn't want to make you feel uncomfortable. Now I probably have."

She shook her head. "Thank you for the compliment." He went back to his driving, but she let her gaze linger on him a little longer. Surprisingly, she didn't feel uncomfortable in his presence. In fact, she was glad he'd be at the dinner tonight. She couldn't imagine facing the family alone. It wasn't like she could invite Gage.

Just the thought of him brought both regret and anger. He'd called her mother to warn her. He was in on it with them against her. Why was it that a complete stranger understood and was trying to help her when the man she'd agreed to marry had betrayed her?

Buck slowed the pickup and turned down a narrow dirt road. The truck's headlights cut a swath through the pines lining each side of the road. They hadn't gone far when the road climbed and a house, aglow with light, appeared against the mountainside.

The log-and-stone house looked so warm and inviting that she felt herself relax a little. As Buck parked and shut off the engine, he glanced over at her and said, "It's going to be fine."

She wasn't sure if he was referring to this dinner or all the rest, but his words helped. "I hope so," she said, surprised when he jumped out and went around to open her door for her as if they were on a date. It was so sweet and gentlemanly that she couldn't help but smile.

MARIBELLE WAS SURPRISED to find Lanny Jackson waiting for her in the living room when she got back to the estate. "Where's Harrison?" she asked, looking around for her husband.

"He's still at work."

The man looked nervous. Had Harrison told him what she'd said about his bodyguard skills? Did she care? "Here." She thrust the box with the gun inside at him. "Get rid of it."

He started to open the box, but her words stopped him.

"You know what's inside. Just make sure it never turns up," she said and handed him a scrap of paper. "You'll need this."

He looked down at the address she'd written down for him and frowned. "What am I supposed to—"

"You'll know what you're supposed to do when you get there. Get rid of the body, and not a word to my husband or you'll be next."

Lanny looked as if he might balk. Or worse—go to Harrison.

She reached into her shoulder bag, glad she hadn't

given the money to Judy. She pulled out half of the cash. If Lanny wanted more, she'd have it ready. If he dared. She thrust the bills at him as her cell phone rang. Waving him away, she turned and started for the stairs, leaving him standing in the foyer staring after her. "Oh, and if you tell my husband, I'll have your eyeballs cut out before I kill you." She glanced back and smiled. The scary thing was he smiled back.

She dismissed him from her mind as she took her husband's call.

"Where have you been?" Harrison demanded.

"Out. Is this about Ansley? Maybe you should talk to your lawyer—you know, be ready. You'll need to buy us a compassionate judge—"

"We don't have enough money to buy a judge for this, Maribelle," he snapped impatiently.

"I'm sure a lawyer will be able to advise us. Maybe I'll call the one that Charlotte Dryer got for her son."

"Please, let me handle it," he said. "I was afraid when I couldn't reach you and Lanny said you weren't home that you might have taken things into your own hands, as you often do."

"I don't want to argue. Could you ask around about sympathetic judges?"

"Maribelle." He apologized for raising his voice. "Please, just trust me."

"In other words, you're going to wait to see what happens. Honestly, Harrison, if this gets out and I'm ostracized by all of our friends, I'll never forgive you. Do you hear me?"

"All our friends?" he said with a sigh. "Who all would that be? We don't have any real friends, Maribelle."

"What are you talking about?" she demanded as she reached the second-floor landing and stopped to catch her breath.

"Nothing. I'm just saying, let me handle it. I've gotten us this far, haven't I?" Silence then, "Mari?"

He hadn't called her that in years. She felt herself soften. "What?" For a moment, she thought he was going to say that he loved her. Did he still love her?

On the other end of the call, she heard him say, "I have to go. I'm taking care of everything. You have to trust me and do nothing. Can you do that?"

A little late for that, she thought as she glanced after Lanny, hoping she could trust him. "Of course. I'm so glad you're handling it."

IN FRONT OF James and Lori's house, Buck offered Ansley a hand as she climbed from the pickup, but as he did, he noticed that she was no longer wearing her engagement ring and froze for a moment. He saw her flush as he raised his gaze to her face. Had she broken off the engagement after what she'd learned about her fiancé? It would be too bad if he didn't get a chance to meet Gage.

He wanted to ask but was afraid of her answer. Maybe she just forgot to put the ring back on. Although he couldn't imagine her going through with a marriage to the man after such a betrayal.

Lori met them at the door, all smiles, and ushered them into the house. He could tell she was doing her best not to stare at Ansley and make this any more uncomfortable than it was.

"Come on in," she said cheerfully. "We're all in the kitchen. Isn't that the way it always works?"

Within moments of entering the house, Ansley didn't know why she'd been nervous. Everyone was so welcoming. James's wife, Lori, introduced her to Tommy's wife, Bella, who handed her a glass of wine.

"This is Carla, Davy's bride," she said. "I'm sure they told you that Davy is on a case down in Wyoming. But you'll meet him soon."

Bella stopped and laughed. "One of us just has to say it, so I guess it's me. You have to be a Colt. The resemblance is just too much."

"I guess we'll see," Ansley said. "Once the DNA report comes back."

"Doesn't matter." Lori put an arm around her shoulders. "We've already made our decision. You're one of us."

The entire dinner was filled with laughter and stories about the Colt brothers as boys. It fascinated her, the kind of childhood they'd all had. They'd gotten to be kids, something she'd missed. With her, it was always, "Now don't you dare get anything on that dress!" Or if she had even a smudge, "Clean up this child—she's disgusting," on her mother's way out the door.

"What hellions they all were," Carla said. "Raised like a pack of wolves."

"We had the perfect childhood," James said.

Tommy agreed. "Just because we had a lot of freedom…"

"To get into trouble," Bella said.

"You should know," her husband said. "You were right there with me."

Ansley could see the love between Tommy and the pregnant Bella. Same with Lori and James. "When are your babies due?"

"I've got months to go," Bella said. "But Lori could pop out those twin boys at any minute." They all laughed.

"Soon," Lori said. "At least, I hope it's soon. It's crowded in there, and they've been kicking up a storm."

Ansley felt as if she'd always known these people. More than ever, she wanted to be part of this family. She feared it would be a mistake to get her hopes up, though, knowing she would be crushed if their DNA wasn't a match.

WILLIE GOT THE call in the middle of dinner. He excused himself and stepped away from the table, mouthing it was work to his wife. Ellie, as he'd always called her, even though her name was actually Eleanor. She nodded and smiled to him, clearly used to this by now as he left the dining room.

He went outside into the spring night. It was early enough in the season that the air was brisk and smelled of pine and new pasture grasses. The sky overhead had filled with stars that now sparkled against an endless, deep blue backdrop. The rising moon rimmed the jagged, dark silhouette of the mountains to the east with gold, while to the west he could see dark clouds. Another spring storm.

"A group of teenagers found a body in a ditch out on the old river road," his deputy told him when he returned the call. "They recognized her. It's Judy Ramsey. She's been shot. A bunch of times, from what I could see. Coroner took her down to the medical center morgue. Pete said the body had been dumped there. Definitely not the crime scene. No tracks other than the ones made by the teenagers. He's going to do the autopsy in the morning."

"Thanks for letting me know," Willie said. "Come daylight, we'll search the area." Though he wondered what good it would do. The teenagers would tell their friends, even though he was sure the deputy had warned them not to. By now, half the town could have driven out there to see the spot.

He shook his head as he disconnected. Judy Ramsey. Lonesome was small enough that most everyone knew each other. Judy had worked as a waitress for years down at the diner. She lived in a small, older house on the west edge of town.

Nothing more he could do tonight, he thought as he went back inside. Still, he wondered who would want to kill Judy Ramsey and dump her body out there off that old highway.

As he started to pocket his phone, he saw the text from the jewelry and engraving store. His day off had gotten crazy after that. He'd forgotten the woman had promised to send the information to him.

He stopped walking to stare at the printing on the form and the signature. The clerk had been right. It was impossible to read. But someone had scribbled in a blank space at the middle of the receipt. *Call*... with a number.

Willie felt his heart rocket in his chest. He knew that number, even though he hadn't seen it in ten years. It was his father's. Del Ransom Colt had bought a necklace for his daughter before she was born and had it engraved with the name DelRae.

ANSLEY COULDN'T REMEMBER enjoying a night more. The Colt family had been so welcoming, the food delicious, and Buck, well, he'd been sweet and supportive. He didn't glance at his phone once—unlike Gage, who was usually glued to his mobile screen.

She stole a look at him, amazed at the circumstances that had brought this cowboy into her life. They'd grown close in a matter of days. She realized that she would trust him with her life and quickly reminded herself that she was just a distraction. She shouldn't read more into it than it was.

Yet she'd never been more aware of a man. The cab of his pickup felt intimate, the darkness beyond the headlights making her feel as if they were the only two people in the world. She fought the urge to lay her head on his broad shoulder and close her eyes as she savored this night.

"Did you have fun?" Buck asked as he drove down the narrow road bordered by tall pines, the boughs black against the midnight blue of the sky overhead.

"I did." She couldn't help smiling. She'd been so nervous, and for no reason, as it turned out. "They are so nice." Her voice broke.

He reached over and took her hand, squeezing it. "I know. I always wanted to be a Colt, too. Fortunately, they adopted me into their family. They're all pretty amazing."

She nodded, afraid to speak for fear it would come out a sob. She'd tried so hard not to get her hopes up. But after tonight, she wanted more than ever for the DNA test results to prove that she was right about what she was feeling. That these were her people. She knew it might not be anything more than wishful thinking on her part. But if she could wish upon a star tonight and make it come true...

"James told me that he's put a rush on the DNA test," he said. "I know the waiting is rough, but we'll know soon."

A part of her wanted to put it off as long as possible for fear that the results would show she was wrong, she thought as he pulled up in front of her motel room door. The night was dark, only a few stars peeking out of the low clouds. The neon motel sign on the highway buzzed, several letters burned-out. It did little to hold back the darkness.

Buck parked and got out, going around the front of the pickup to open her door. It had felt like a date all night. She'd felt such a rush of warmth whenever she looked at him and found him looking back, smiling. *Don't get attached*, she told herself. *Not to the Colts, definitely not to Buck Crawford. Your life is miles away, and when this over, even if you are a Colt...*

As he opened her door, he took her arm. She stepped out and directly into his arms. She looked up into his eyes in surprise. What she saw there made her heart hammer in her chest and her breath catch. It happened so quickly, she wasn't sure who initiated the kiss—just that she found herself pulled even closer, her lips parting, her whole body wanting this.

"Buck." The word came out as a breathless plea as she looked into his eyes and drew back, shaken by her body's reaction to the kiss.

BUCK IMMEDIATELY HELD up his hands in surrender as their gazes locked. "I'm sorry. I don't know what I was—" He let out a curse. "No, I'm not sorry." Before he could stop himself, he closed the space between them again and pulled her into his arms. This time there was nothing tentative about the kiss. It was all passion, all desire, all need.

He felt her open up to him, heard a whispered groan as her body came to his with a need almost matching his own. He deepened the kiss, drawing her up against him, feeling her soft, full breasts against his chest, desperately wanting to sweep her up and carry her inside and make love to her.

But she wasn't his. Not yet. He drew back from the kiss. "I've wanted to do that almost from the moment I laid eyes on you." His gaze bored into hers. But now, after having her in his arms, feeling her respond to his mouth on hers, he wanted a damned sight more, and that scared the bejesus out of him.

He could see her trembling, as if she was as unsteady on her feet as he was. But he could also see the heat of desire in her eyes, even as she took a step back. "I'm the one who's sorry. I shouldn't have let myself get carried away like that. I'm *engaged*." The last word sounded strangled.

"Are you?" He glanced at her bare finger. "Are you still planning to marry him?"

Ansley took a breath and let it out slowly before her gaze locked with his again. "So much has happened so fast. I… I feel as if I can't trust any of my feelings."

He cocked his head at her and then laughed. "Boy howdy. I'm the one who should be pulling back the reins, yelling whoa." He dragged off his Stetson and raked a hand through his hair. "The last woman I fell in love with turned out to be a psychopath. She damned near killed me. I swore…" He didn't finish that thought. "I should get you inside. I can feel a storm coming."

"Buck." What had she planned to say? Hadn't the way she'd kissed him said it all? She moved toward her motel room, still seeming unsteady on her feet. He had felt her passion, seen it in her eyes. He mentally kicked himself for his impulsive behavior. It wasn't like him.

He watched her open the motel room door and go inside. She hesitated for a moment at the door, as if wanting to say something, but then quickly closed it. He heard her turn the lock.

Turning, he walked back to his pickup, fighting the mix of emotions coursing through him. He'd thrown caution to the wind. What had he been thinking? Of course he was attracted to her. She was beautiful. He'd wanted to kiss her and make love to her, but that hadn't been coming from his head. She was the last thing he needed. To make matters worse, his future was up in the air right now. What would a woman like her want with an unemployed cowboy with a saddlebag full of baggage from his past?

Chapter Thirteen

Ansley stepped into her motel room, closed the door and leaned against it. Her whole body tingled. She could feel the weight of her breasts, the nipples hard and aching. The kiss had taken her by surprise, but not just because it had been unexpected. She felt her face heat at the memory of how she'd kissed him back.

The passion she'd felt. Where had that come from? She'd never felt that kind of intensity, that kind of need with Gage. But then, he'd never kissed her like that. She closed her eyes, remembering the feel of her body against Buck's. She'd never wanted anyone the way she had the cowboy.

Just the thought of his words… His confession, his desire for her. How had she let this happen? She was still engaged. She barely knew this cowboy. She couldn't trust the emotions raging through her right now.

Yet no one had ever kissed her like that. No one had ever made her feel like that.

Ansley told herself that she needed sleep and blamed the magic of the night for her confused feelings. Dinner with the Colts had been so enjoyable. She couldn't remember when she'd had that much fun. That's how she'd ended up in Buck's arms. She'd been caught up in all these new feelings.

She still felt so worked up, she doubted she was going to be able to sleep even after her shower. She kept going over the night, wrapped in the warmth of the Colt family. As she got ready for bed, she reminded herself that she might not be a Colt. That when the DNA results came back, it could burst this bubble she was in right now. Climbing into bed, she tried not to think about what would happen if she wasn't really part of the Colt family.

Realizing she was trying to think about anything but Buck Crawford, she turned her thoughts to the mystery woman she was searching for. She still didn't know who her birth mother was. Or her father, for that matter. Del Ransom Colt? Maybe not. She thought about Judy Ramsey. Was she her birth mother? Tomorrow, she would go by the woman's house again.

Maybe she was getting close to solving this, she thought as she lay in the darkness staring up at the cracked ceiling of the old motel room. Her thoughts kept circling back to dinner tonight, though, and the Colts and Buck and his kisses.

Had he been caught up in the magic of the night as well? Was that why he'd kissed her, why he'd said what he did? She told herself that he would feel differently in the morning. They would probably both pretend the kisses had never happened.

Just as she was starting to drift off, she heard footfalls outside her door. She froze as they were followed, closer, by a whispered noise. As the footfalls retreated, she turned on the light and saw that someone had pushed an envelope under her door.

BUCK FOUND JAMES waiting for him at the office. He'd said he needed to talk to him but privately after dinner. He'd suggested they meet at the office. Kissing Ansley still simmering in his blood and his brain, he took a chair across the big oak desk from James. He felt as if he'd taken a beating today. He should go home to the ranch, but he had to know what was up. "Any word on who was driving the pickup borrowed from Mark's lot?"

"He said he talked to his wife. She lent the pickup to Penny Graves down at city hall. You know her?"

Buck nodded. "Why would she borrow it?"

"Said her rig was broke down and needed it to get to work. Said she left the keys in it, parked outside city hall, because she thought Mark was going to pick it up. Sounds like someone borrowed it. Mark says it's back on the lot."

"Why would Penny Graves follow Ansley to Bozeman?" he asked, more to himself than James.

"Doubt she would. Could have been anyone driving it, even some kid just screwing around."

"I suppose," Buck said. "Unless she borrowed the pickup for someone else."

James rose. "I'm glad you stopped by. I wanted to talk to you," his friend said. "Come on." He led Buck upstairs, stopping just long enough to pull a couple of beers from the apartment refrigerator before taking the stairs to the roof.

James handed him a beer and motioned to one of the folding beach chairs. Only a few lights lit the main drag of Lonesome. Residents often joked that the sidewalks rolled up early in the evening when they described Lonesome. Behind the town, the dense pines added their scents to the night breeze.

Buck had to smile as he opened his beer, took a seat and stared up at the darkening night sky filled with stars. He and his friends had come up here often as teens. He'd missed those nights. He pulled off his Stetson, set it aside and leaned back as he took a drink of the cold beer. After the day he'd had, it tasted wonderful. And it was clear that James had something on his mind.

"As you know, when I came back to town, mostly to heal from my last rodeo ride, and got involved with Dad's last investigation, I didn't have plans to be a private investigator," his friend began. "Even when I got hooked on the job, I never thought I could make a go of it. Then Tommy wanted in and then Davy…"

Buck started to speak, but James cut him off. "The point is, Colt Brothers Investigation has taken off. We're getting calls from all over the Northwest. We could use help from someone who is more qualified than any of us."

"You know someone like that?" Buck asked, tongue in cheek.

"I'm serious. You don't want to raise rough stock, even if your dad and brother needed your help, and I suspect you don't want to be a highway patrolman again. Am I right?"

Buck looked down at his boots. "I appreciate the offer, but—"

"You'd be doing us a favor. I did save your life that time." His old friend looked up and grinned.

"I was wondering how long it would be before you cashed in on that," Buck said.

"How about you try it out for a while?" James suggested. "See if you like it. See if you like working with us." He shrugged. "Either way, no hard feelings. Debt paid." He grinned to let him know he was kidding about the debt. "I was hoping you'd work the Ansley Brookshire case with us." He gave Buck a side-eye. "Unless you aren't interested."

Buck chuckled. "I admit it's tempting, but maybe that's why I should give it a wide berth."

James shook his head. "You need to forgive yourself for falling in love with the wrong woman."

He snorted at that. "If anyone should have known better, it was me."

It was James's turn to laugh. "What makes you so much smarter than the rest of us when it comes to women?"

"Because I was a cop," he snapped. "A damned good one, I'm told. I should have seen it. I should have sensed it. I should have heard it the moment she opened her mouth."

"Yep, psychopaths have such obvious tells."

Buck took a drink of his beer, licking the foam from his lips. The midnight blue canvas was alive with stars. A breeze stirred his hair. When had he let it get so long? Not that it mattered. He'd come home to the ranch, his safe place, and yet the woman of his nightmares had followed him, reminding him that he would never be free of her. Look how suspicious he was of Ansley Brookshire. How could he ever trust his judgment when it came to anyone—especially women—ever again?

"You'll get past it," James said quietly, his gaze skyward.

Buck didn't express his doubts. He didn't have to. His friend knew him too well.

"Why do you think Willie never wanted to fall in love? Then he met Ellie. You think I wasn't terrified of the feelings Lori stirred up in me?" James chuckled. "Everything about it was wrong, and at the worst time of my life, I thought." He glanced over at Buck. "You're dealing with a lot. Almost dying does something to you, no doubt about that. Willie almost drowned twice. Who knows if he'll ever go back in the water." He laughed. "But he loves the hell out of Ellie. That he'll never regret."

Buck shook his head, unable to imagine surrendering to that kind of love. "I thought we were talking about a job."

"We are. You need something to challenge you. But we also could use your help with this case, especially going up against Harrison Brookshire. You know Lonesome and this county. We're pretty sure that Ansley wasn't born in a hospital. That means either a home birth or a midwife. Someone in this town knows."

"By the way, Ansley and I talked to Toni down at the yarn shop again. She thinks Judy Ramsey bought the yarn. We went by her house. She wasn't around. You want me to keep beating the bushes?"

James shook his head. "I want you to make sure Ansley is okay. She trusts you. I have faith in you keeping her safe until we get to the bottom of this."

That made him want to laugh. He wasn't sure she was safe at all around him. He knew damned well that he wasn't safe with her. "After tonight, you have to know there is no getting rid of her—even if it turns out your DNA doesn't match. The wives all loved her. They've already adopted her into the family," Buck said.

"The women definitely did take to her," James said. "Ansley Brookshire is quite captivating, but then, I don't have to tell you that, do I."

Buck stared up at the stars, enjoying the Montana spring evening even though it was far from warm. He drank his beer and thought about Ansley in his arms, his mouth on hers. He was already in over his head, in deep in this when it came to the woman—and that worried the hell out of him.

ANSLEY FROZE FOR a moment at the sight of the white envelope lying just inside her door. She listened but heard no sound outside her motel room. Why hadn't she jumped up, run to open the door and tried to see who'd left it? Because she was wearing nothing but one of the large, worn T-shirts she slept in—not to mention that she'd been too surprised to react.

It might be something from Buck. Apologizing for kissing her? Seemed unlikely. Or something from one of the Colts. Maybe news.

Frowning, she stepped toward the white envelope and bent down to pick it up. She felt a shiver and knew it wasn't from Buck or the Colts about her case. It was something else, something she felt instinctively that she wasn't going to like.

She turned the envelope over. It wasn't sealed. She slowly lifted the flap. There appeared to be a single sheet of note paper inside. She carefully pulled it out, trying not to leave her fingerprints. As it fell open, she caught sight of the words inside. The letters appeared to have been cut from a magazine.

GO HoMe bEfORe iTs ToO lATe

She stared at the words, her heart in her throat, before she carried the note over to the small desk and dropped both the note and the envelope. Her first instinct was to call Buck, but she'd relied on him too much already. James? She glanced at the time. Too late. It would keep until tomorrow. But she had to admit she was scared. She'd never dreamed that looking for her birth mother would elicit this kind of response.

What she couldn't understand was who was behind this—and why. Judy Ramsey? Had Toni or someone else warned her that Ansley wanted to see her? There was no way Maribelle would take the time to cut out each letter and glue it to a sheet of note paper—let alone drive to Lonesome to shove it under her motel room door. In the first place, her adoptive mother wouldn't know where she was staying.

But someone did. Lanny Jackson? Didn't seem his style. Then who?

She closed her eyes for a moment, unable to accept that maybe her birth mother didn't want to be found. She'd given up her baby to Maribelle. That alone told Ansley that the woman might have cared enough to learn to knit and make her a baby blanket and buy a few clothes, but ultimately, she hadn't wanted her. Was she now worried that her daughter was about to expose her secret?

Ansley realized she had no idea who was threatening her or how serious they might be. She checked the lock on the motel room door and shoved a chair under the knob. There was no chance she was going to get any sleep.

ON THE DRIVE home to the ranch, Buck got the call. He'd been mentally kicking himself, not just for kissing Ansley but for telling her how badly he'd want to kiss her. He wouldn't be surprised if she wanted nothing more to do with him. He was a bigger fool than even he thought if he lost the job with the Colt brothers. He wanted it—at least temporarily.

"Didn't you tell me that Toni's sure the woman who bought the yarn was Judy Ramsey?" James asked. Buck could hear Tommy and Davy arguing in the background, with Willie trying to break them up.

"She's pretty sure, why?"

"Willie's here. Judy Ramsey was found murdered earlier tonight. Shot, and more than once."

Buck slowed the pickup as he took in this information. "You think it's possible that she's Ansley birth mother and this is somehow connected?"

"I don't know. But I'll tell Willie and the others what you told me. If Ansley really is our half sister..." James sighed. "Dad and Judy?" In the background, Buck heard Willie telling him not to jump to conclusions. "Talk in the morning."

"Yeah, and James...? I'll take the job. At least temporarily. If it's okay with Ansley."

"Right. Glad to hear that."

He had a bad thought. "I left Ansley at the motel. She should be safe, right?"

"I'll ask Willie to have a deputy drive by during the night," James said.

He disconnected, his thoughts whirling. Judy Ramsey was dead. Murdered. He thought of how Harrison and Maribelle Brookshire had been one step ahead of them thanks to the tracking devices they'd put on their daughter's phone and SUV with the help of her fiancé.

Had Judy Ramsey been killed because he and Ansley wanted to talk to her? If so, they'd had Lanny Jackson take care of it, he told himself. He wondered when he and the burly bodyguard would cross paths again. Soon, he figured, hoping he would be ready as he drove the rest of the way to the ranch.

As he parked and climbed out of his pickup, he spotted his father sitting in the dark on the porch. "Have a nice night?" Wendell Crawford asked as Buck climbed the steps to join him.

He nodded and sat down in one of the porch chairs

next to him to look out at the darkness. He could smell the coming thunderstorm on the night air and feel the chill.

"You've been spending quite a lot of time in town lately," his father said. "Makes me wonder if there's a woman who's caught your eye."

Buck chuckled. His father could read him like an open book and always had. "I'm helping James with a case, and yes, there is a woman involved." Out of the corner of his eye, he saw the older man nod and knew he must have heard the scuttlebutt.

"I suspected it might be something like that," his dad said. "Heard a little about it from a breeder who stopped by. A young woman looking for her birth mother."

Still, he couldn't believe the way news traveled in this county. Ranches could be miles from town, and yet word managed to get there. He wondered how much his father had heard. "James offered me a job. Temporarily, while I figure some things out." He knew his father had been worried about him. "I've taken it."

"To work on this case." Wendell Crawford nodded and picked up his iced tea from the small table next to his chair to take a drink. "There's more tea if you're interested."

"I'm fine. Not sure how much you've heard, but she could be related to the Colts." Silence from his father. "You were friends with Del Ransom Colt," he said, not sure how to ask what he needed to know. "After his wife died, was there someone else?"

"He was pretty busy raising four boys."

Buck gave him a side-eye. "*Raising* might not be

the right word. You didn't deny that there might have been a woman."

"Not necessarily. Some of us, when we've had the best, we know we can never love another woman like that again. So we don't try."

Buck would love for his father to find someone again. His mother had been gone for seven years now, but while he couldn't see his father marrying again, Buck would have liked for him to at least have a female companion.

"This woman thinks she's your friends' half sister, I heard," Wendell said.

"We're waiting on the DNA test results, but the first time I saw her, there was something so familiar about her. There's something else." He hesitated. "You'll hear about this soon enough. Judy Ramsey was found murdered tonight. There's a chance she's the birth mother."

His father took a sip of his iced tea, seemed to give it some thought before he put down the glass and said, "My first instinct is that Del wouldn't have gotten involved again—especially that quickly. Isn't this woman claiming to be their sister about Davy's age?" Buck nodded. "But maybe I'm going with my own feeling after I lost your mother." His father shook his head. "No one could replace her. But as for Del…" He chuckled. "Can't see him with Judy Ramsey, though. But then I couldn't see him with Penny Graves, either."

"Penny Graves? The woman who works at the mayor's office?" Interesting, since whoever had followed Ansley to Brookshire Estate in the borrowed pickup had been from the mayor's office, apparently.

His father nodded slowly. "I don't like spreading rumors, but if I hadn't seen them together myself... I guess he and Penny were seen together more than a few times." Buck heard the hesitation in his father's voice and waited. "If they had a relationship, it was a rocky one, from what I saw. You think Penny could be this young woman's mother?"

"That's just it—we have no idea at this point." He sat for a few minutes, listening to the night sounds. "I suppose there are always women who are interested in a widower," Buck said, thinking of his father now more than Del.

Wendell laughed. "Some believe they can make you love again, heal your heart, fill that place. They bring pies and casseroles. They do their best to catch your eye. Most are just lonely. Believe it or not, there were even some who set their sights on me, and I'm not half as good-looking or exciting as Del Colt."

Buck laughed. "I've seen how Angie Fredericks always saves you a spot next to her at church and Emily Larson brings your favorite bars for after the service. You've still got it."

His father chuckled to himself. "None of them can hold a candle to your mother. Not their fault. Just not interested. But Del... His wife was sick for so long, in and out of the hospital. He was sole guardian to those boys. He had to have been lonely, though, needing someone. How far it went, who knows."

"Can you think of anyone else Del might have been involved with?" Buck asked, seeing that his father had someone in mind.

Wendell shook his head before turning to him. "I'm more worried about the woman in your life than Del's," his father said changing the subject. "Just be careful. Mind your heart, son. Since you were a boy, you always tried to help anyone in need, anyone in trouble. You brought home everything from birds with broken wings to stray dogs and cats that looked hungry."

"If you're saying I'm a bleeding heart… Ansley Brookshire is far from a stray cat. And I don't have designs on her."

His father laughed. "I'm just saying you're a wonderful son with a big heart and a lot of compassion for others. Those are not shortcomings." He finished his tea and rose, taking the empty glass with him. "But like you said, until you get the DNA results, you can't even be sure who this woman is. She might not be related to anyone in the county—maybe especially the Colts." He felt his father's gaze on him. "But that isn't going to make a difference to you, is it."

Chapter Fourteen

Ansley came out of a deep, dark sleep filled with nightmares. She sat bolt upright in bed. Scared, she frantically searched the small motel room before she realized her cell was ringing and that's what had awakened her.

She glanced at her phone next to her bed and the time. Who would be calling this early? Buck? James? Had something happened? "Hello?" She felt a jolt as she heard Gage's voice.

"We need to talk."

She couldn't help think about all the messages she'd left him and her attempts to reach him yesterday. "At this hour? What's wrong?"

"How can you even ask that?" he demanded. "Do you know what you're doing to me?"

She groaned inwardly. Seriously? This was about her finding her birth mother? This really wasn't the time, not after her scare last night with the threatening note.

"This really has nothing to do with you." The moment the words were out of her mouth, she regretted them. Buck had made her question Gage's loyalty to her. Not that she hadn't worried that he'd called her mother

to warn her about the photo. She hadn't wanted to believe it. Still didn't. It was just a photo. A photo that
wasn't even proof.

"Nothing to do with me?" He sounded both shocked
and hurt.

"You know what I mean."

"No, I don't think I do. Just open the door so we can
talk face-to-face."

Open the door? She glanced at her motel room door.
"Where are you?" she asked, her voice strained at the
thought that he was out there.

"Right outside."

Had he been out there last night, shoving an envelope under her door?

"You tracked me down?" Now fully awake, she felt
a rush of anger.

"Ansley, please. Just open the door. I drove all the
way up here to talk to you—and not through a motel
room door."

She disconnected. He'd tracked her down without
the help of the tracking devices Buck had removed. Or
were there others he'd missed?

Still stunned and upset, she slid out of bed and
quickly pulled on clothes before going to the door and
throwing it open. Gage stood just outside, looking impatient and out of sorts. "What are you doing here?"
she demanded.

"Hoping to talk some sense into you," he snapped
as he pushed past her and into the room.

Ansley felt her hackles rise as she closed the door and
turned to face him. Fiancé or not, she felt bullied, and

she didn't like it. "You could have called before driving up, and I would have saved you the trip."

His expression softened. "I'm sorry. I've just been so worried about you." He glanced around the sparse furnishings of the motel room. "This was the best you could do?"

"Gage—"

He held up his hands. "Sorry, but could we at least get out of this depressing room and go across the street to that café? I could use some coffee. We can talk. You can tell me what's going on with you."

She took a breath and let it out. Coffee right now sounded good. She also felt strangely uncomfortable in this motel room with him—as uncomfortable as he looked. "Just give me a minute. You can wait outside if it makes you feel better." He nodded, and she went into the bathroom to freshen up.

All she could think about was that she'd kissed Buck and now Gage was here. She felt disloyal, and yet she wasn't sorry about the kiss, which made her feel worse. Gage was *here*. She was trying to get her mind around that. She thought about the note pushed under her door. Had he driven up this morning? Or did he come up last night?

She hated even thinking that he might have lied about that.

As she stepped out of the bathroom, she was surprised to see that Gage hadn't gone outside. He was standing next to her bed, holding the framed photograph of the Colt brothers. "What are you doing in my purse?"

"I saw the edge of the frame sticking out. I was curious." He held it up, then reached for the one of her that he'd also taken out of her purse. "This is the photo you just had to have from the house?"

"If you compare the two…"

Gage frowned. "Compare them why?" He swore. "You think you're related to these…these…boys?"

She instantly felt the need to defend the Colts. "They're successful men now."

"I hope they discovered soap." Shaking his head, he met her gaze. "You don't really want to be related to some backwoods cowboys rather than accept Maribelle and Harrison Brookshire as your family, do you?"

"I want to know the truth." She stepped to the end table where she'd left her shoulder bag. Picking it up, she reached for the framed photos. "Do you really not see the resemblance from the photo when I was five?" He shook his head, looking at her as if she'd lost her mind. "Then why was it that you and Maribelle were so determined that I not take it?"

He stared at her blankly. "What are you talking about?"

"That photo in your hand of me. It's the one I told you I was getting from the house. But when I arrived, the photo wasn't where it was always kept. Maribelle had hidden it right before I got there. You called her and told her I was coming, didn't you?"

"I don't even remember you mentioning a photograph. I was at work. I was busy. I certainly didn't remember some photo of you when you were five. You think I called your mother?"

She heard the answer in his voice, in his overworked denial. She glared at him. "Give me the photos."

He did, though reluctantly. "You don't know what you're saying. You know how you are before you have your coffee in the morning. Come on—I didn't come here to argue. I really wanted to see you and find out what's going on."

Ansley ground her teeth. She'd just bet he did, since Buck had removed the tracking devices from her phone and vehicle. It wouldn't have been that hard for him to find her, since her SUV was parked right outside and the motel was on the main drag.

But she told herself that he was right about one thing. Coffee. She needed it before she said what she really thought.

Neither of them spoke again until the waitress put two cups of coffee and menus in front of them at a booth in the corner of the café. They both drank, avoiding each other's gazes for a few minutes. When she finally looked at him, she saw the truth on his face as clearly as she saw it in his rumpled suit. "You lied about calling my mother about the photo, and you didn't drive up this morning."

He started to argue, then seemed to change his mind. "Everything I've done was for your own good." He rushed on as he saw her angry expression. "I don't think you realize the damage you are doing to your life. You have two amazing parents who wanted you and gave you everything. How can you throw all that away for some fantasy family? How can you afford to?"

"I started my business without any help from them."

She'd begun making jewelry at a young age, selling it to friends. The business had kept growing along with her skills. "I made a success out of it on my own. I can afford to do whatever I want."

"Yes, yes, I know. You're a self-made woman. You've told me that enough times. Whereas I work for my father. You must think I'm a real sellout, huh."

"I'm not the one telling you how to live your life."

His face flushed for a moment as the waitress refilled their cups and left. He took a drink of his coffee, setting the cup down a little too hard and splashing some on the table. He grabbed a napkin and began to dab at the spill. "Maybe I don't want to always work for my father. Maybe I haven't had the privileges you have taken for granted. Maybe someday I'd like a helping hand up, since I'm not as…talented as you are."

She took a sip of her coffee before she said, "Let's be clear, you're talking about my inheritance."

He met her gaze, both hands wrapped around his coffee cup. "See, that's exactly what I mean. You've always had anything you wanted, so it's easy for you to scoff at a fortune."

"I didn't have everything I always wanted. I actually wanted a family like yours."

His laugh was laced with bitterness. "You don't have a clue."

"Maybe not," she agreed after consuming more coffee. She could feel the caffeine doing its job. She was waking up more—and not just from a night's sleep. "But I am starting to see a lot of things more clearly." She held his gaze, seeing the real Gage Sheridan. He'd always been impressed by the Brookshire lifestyle. Clearly, he wanted it more than he wanted anything else—her included. "As a matter of fact, I've needed to talk to you, so I'm glad you drove up. Slept in your car, did you?"

He didn't deny it. He must have been parked down the street, waiting for her to come back from her dinner. Had he seen the kisses between her and Buck? Or had he fallen asleep and that's why she hadn't known he was here until this morning? No, she thought, he'd woken up just long enough to slide the envelope under her door. He must have had his assistant at work cut and glue the letters from the magazine, though. Unless it really had been from someone else.

She reached into her purse, dug to the bottom and pulled out the engagement ring. "All of this has made me realize—"

"What the hell?" He seemed to start as he stared at her left hand, then at the ring she put down on the table between them. "When did you stop wearing your engagement ring?" His gaze flew back to her face. "Is this about that cowboy? I saw the two of you last night."

"Seems you have been keeping track of me for some time," she said. "That cowboy is a former law officer. He found the tracking devices on my SUV and on my phone. But you wouldn't know anything about that, right?"

"No." He shook his head, his Adam's apple working furiously. "You are not breaking up with me. Your mother's right. You've lost your mind and need professional help. She wanted to get you locked up, but I told her I would try to talk some sense into you—"

"My mind is just fine." She realized with a jolt that she hadn't seen the threatening note where she'd left it on the desk back in the motel. "Did you take that note that was in my room?"

He frowned. "Why would I take—"

She cursed under her breath as she got to her feet. "You can tell Maribelle that I'm just fine. As for you... The engagement is off. Please don't ever contact me again."

He glanced at the ring, then at her, and shook his head. "You'll change your mind. You'll see that everything I've done was to save you. You wouldn't be happy with some cowboy."

"Not that it is your business any longer," she said, thinking of Buck's kiss. It wasn't about the cowboy. The kiss had only made her more confident that Gage wasn't the man for her. She just hadn't admitted it to herself after he'd been against her finding her birth mother. She'd known then that he didn't understand her need—or care. He'd only been worried about her getting cut out of the Brookshire inheritance.

Her cell phone rang. She saw it was James.

"Don't answer it," Gage snapped. "We aren't done here."

"Hello, James," she said into the phone, stepping back as her ex-fiancé tried to take the phone from her hand. She turned her back on him. "The DNA test results are back? I'll be right there." She disconnected and turned to look at Gage.

He had his phone out but now pocketed it. He looked flushed, as if she'd caught him texting someone behind her back.

"I'm sure you've already let them know, but just in case you haven't, I'm going to find out the truth," she said. "You and Maribelle and Harrison are going to have to accept it."

He shook his head. "You're making a huge mistake."

"No, I did that when I agreed to marry you," she said and walked out.

WILLIE ENTERED THE local medical center, anxious to talk to the coroner. The center served the community with limited staff and also provided a morgue and autopsy room in the basement.

He nodded to the physician's assistant who was busy stitching up a teenage boy in the ER and headed for the basement. He found the coroner standing in front of a metal table on which Judy Ramsey's body now rested. Was this woman Ansley's birth mother? It sure looked that way. Earlier, Tommy had called to tell him that nearly twenty-nine years ago, Judy Ramsey had come into enough money to put a down payment on the old house she lived in on the edge of town.

"Mornin', Pete," he said as he stepped into the room, but kept his distance. He didn't want to have to suit up unless necessary. "Gunshot wounds?"

"Looks like five from a .45. I've been able to retrieve one." He pointed to a small metal dish with a blood-coated slug lying in it. "All the shots were close range. No defensive wounds."

"So more than likely she knew her killer," Willie said. "Any idea where she was killed?"

"Outside. There was caked dirt on the bottom of her shoes, different from the soil where the body was dumped." The sheriff raised an eyebrow. "I know my dirt," Pete said. "She was killed closer to the river." Willie didn't doubt that Pete knew what he was talking about, since he'd trained in forensics before moving to Lonesome to semiretire. "She wasn't dressed for an early-spring swim in the river. Had she been to work that day?"

Willie shook his head. "She'd injured her leg at work, was off for a while."

"She was wearing makeup—more than she usually wore at the café," Pete said.

Willie took that in as he marveled at how observant the man was. "A date out by the river?"

"Could be." Pete picked up a small glass dish. "She had a splinter in her hand. The wood is weathered but has some old green paint on it, like from a picnic table."

"I'll have my deputies look for old, weathered once-green picnic tables down that way," the sheriff said. "What else can you tell me?"

"She broke her arm when she was young, after all these years on her feet, she has varicose veins, and she's been through menopause and had a terrible diet."

Willie shook his head, chuckling. "Can you tell me if she gave birth? There's a woman looking for her mother." He'd been joking so was surprised when Pete looked up.

"This woman has never given birth to a child."

He stared at him. "You can be that sure?"

The coroner nodded. "Sorry, but she's not the woman you're looking for."

Willie's cell phone rang. He excused himself and took the call out in the hall. Deputy Chris Fraser sounded excited. "We have her DNA. Judy Ramsey's. From when she was arrested for a DUI. Do you want me to let the lab know?"

"Thanks, but it won't be necessary now." He told him to take another deputy and drive along the old river road looking for a weathered once-green wooden picnic table. "There's a good chance it's the murder scene."

His phone rang. Willie got as far as his patrol SUV when a call came in from Chris. He was anxious to get to Bozeman, worried about Buck and Ansley.

"Judy Ramsey's neighbor says Judy left a letter with her years ago," the deputy told him. "She thinks it might be important—thinks Judy was worried about someone killing her. I didn't open the envelope, just put it in an evidence bag. I'm at your office."

"I'm on my way," Willie said and drove the few blocks to the sheriff's department. As he walked in, the deputy held up an evidence bag with a yellowed envelope inside. Taking it, he saw that Judy had apparently written "In Case I'm Dead" on the outside.

The deputy said, "Didn't even touch it. I had her drop it into the bag."

Willie nodded and took it into his office. Taking gloves from his drawer, he pulled them on and opened the bag to take out the letter. The handwriting was sloppy, as if she'd been hurried, many of the words

misspelled. But still, he didn't have any trouble under-
standing what was written.

The first two lines sent his pulse pounding.

*DelRae, if you red this, I'm so sorry. I shoold
never have gave you to that woman. There is
a place in hell wating for me. After what I did.
Things didn't go rite. I thought it was the best
thing. No one wood get hurt—until I found out I
wasn't pregnant. Female promblems.*

*I was despurate. She'd given me $50,000 for
a baby girl. What was I goin todo? I coudn't tell
her the truth. I did what I had to do. I told meself
I was helpin out someone in trouble. That I was
savin the baby.*

*Now I'm scard. I don't trust her. I swor I'd nevr
tell, but I don't think she beleeves me.*

*That's why I'm writin this down. Mariblle
Brookshire will kill me to keep the secret. But the
laugh is on her. She don't even no that the baby I
sold her want even mine. No one nos.*

His heart hammered against his ribs as he reread it.
No mistaking the words. Judy Ramsey had sold a baby
to Maribelle Brookshire, a baby she'd called DelRae.
But if she hadn't been pregnant, then where did she
get a baby? And why name the infant DelRae—after
her father?

There was a large missing piece of this puzzle—
DelRae's mother, the one who'd given birth to her.

Meanwhile, Willie had to deal with the information

he had. Judy Ramsey was dead and had named Maribelle as her killer. But why kill her? Because Ansley was searching for her birth mother and Maribelle was determined that Ansley never find her. He thought about James saying that Judy's name kept coming up in the investigation. It was just a matter of time before they ended up at her door to question her. Maribelle must have realized that.

Judy's fears had apparently been warranted. If Maribelle had killed her. Willie let out a curse. What the hell was he going to do with this? He knew that the letter wouldn't be enough evidence. Not against Mrs. Harrison Brookshire.

He thought of Ansley and how she was going to take this news. Willie pulled out his phone and called the county attorney. "We have a big problem. I'm on my way over." He bagged the letter again, afraid none of this would hold up in court against a Brookshire.

He'd barely disconnected when he got another call. He saw it was his brother James. "What's up?"

ANSLEY FELT THE tension in the room the moment she walked in the Colt Brothers Investigation office. James was sitting behind the big oak desk. Tommy and Davy had pulled up five chairs in front of it and taken two of them. Buck had been waiting by the door. As Ansley sat down in one chair, Buck took the chair next to her.

After a few moments with no one speaking, Willie came through the door. James motioned to the last empty chair, but he shook his head and opted to stand against the wall near the door.

James cleared his throat before explaining that the lab had tested Ansley's DNA taken from her blood sample and compared it to Willie's, which was on file. "I asked for confirmation in writing," he said. "I haven't opened it. I thought we should all be here when I did."

"Just get on with it," Willie snapped, crossing his arms as he leaned against the wall.

Ansley swallowed as she looked from one face to another, suddenly terrified that she was wrong. After the other night at James and Lori's house, she felt like part of the family. What if they'd all been wrong about that? To find four brothers and their wives, only to lose them all again, would be a crushing blow. Her eyes burned. She blinked to hold back tears as James picked up the letter opener.

Holding her breath, she watched as he hesitated. She wanted this too badly, she thought as she looked at the official envelope lying on the big oak desk.

Beside her, Buck took her hand and squeezed it. He'd said that no matter what she found out, she already felt like part of the Colt family—and his own. But they both knew it wouldn't be the same. The disappointment would be excruciating.

"Just rip off the bandage," Willie said with a groan.

James picked up the envelope. He sliced the edge open and, taking a breath, pulled out the report. He read silently for a moment, Willie moving to read over his shoulder.

Ansley watched James's face. He was the one who'd been most skeptical about her being his half sister. But she also knew why he was hoping that she was wrong, because of his father. Possibly *their* father, Del.

When he looked up at her, he broke into the first genuine smile she'd seen on his face when he looked at her. Her heart dropped. *I'm not his sister, I'm not his blood, I'm a fraud, just as he's always suspected.*

"Welcome to the family, sis," he said.

For a moment, she thought she'd misunderstood. This time there was no holding back the tears. "It's true? I'm a Colt?"

He nodded, still smiling, as he opened the desk drawer and pulled out a bottle of blackberry brandy and some small paper cups.

Buck was squeezing her hand as they all rose to their feet. Tommy hugged her, Willie gave her a high five, Davy congratulated her and James handed her a paper cup half-full of brandy.

"We try to only drink this when we have something to celebrate," James said as he passed out the other cups, then held his up. "Welcome, although a lot of people wouldn't think finding out that you're related the wild Colt brothers is anything to celebrate."

They laughed, held up their cups and all drank.

"Now, we just need to find your mother," James said as the room turned more somber. "At least now we know who your father is."

Chapter Fifteen

Ansley felt as if she were in a dream. She had family. Four half brothers and their wives. James had called home before she'd left the office. Apparently, Lori, Bella, Ellie and Carla had been waiting for the news. She heard cheering as James held the phone away from his ear.

She realized that she couldn't be happier. James had said that Bella was planning a party to celebrate out at the ranch. Ansley was still trying to take it all in. She'd fought so hard not to get her hopes up. Yet she had, and now it was true. She was a Colt. Del Ransom Colt had been her father.

There was only one piece missing—her birth mother. As she walked toward her motel room just down the street, she couldn't help the feeling that her mother was here in Lonesome and had been all these years.

"Ansley?"

She turned instinctively, a smile already curving her mouth upward before she realized who it was who'd called after her. "Gage, I thought you left."

"We didn't get to finish our talk." He eyed her. "So the news must have been good."

"I'm a Colt. The Colt brothers are my half brothers."
He laughed. "I don't know what to say."

"How about 'I'm happy for you' to start with? I've found my family, and I couldn't be happier."

He stared at her, shaking his head. "Where does that leave Maribelle and Harrison?"

"They're still my adoptive parents, and I'm grateful for everything they did for me. But it doesn't change my need to find my birth mother. So you can report back to them and tell them that I'm not quitting my search." She started to turn, but he grabbed her arm. She jerked free, turning to glare at him. "It's over, Gage. Maybe Maribelle will adopt you. Goodbye."

She started down the street again when she heard the roar of an engine followed by the screech of brakes as a white van pulled up next to the curb. Before she could move, two men in white coats jumped out. She tried to scream for help as they grabbed her, but one of them had covered her mouth with his gloved hand. She felt the jab of a needle in her arm as she was lifted off her feet and into the open side door of the van.

Just before the drug she'd been injected with began to knock her out, she looked back and saw Gage standing on the sidewalk. She could tell from his expression that this had all been planned, and he'd been in on it. The last thing she saw was his smug face as her body went limp on the van floor and the door slammed shut with the same speed as her eyelids.

After Ansley left, Willie asked Buck and his brothers to stay. "Judy Ramsey isn't Ansley's birth mother.

I didn't want to hit her with the news yet." He quickly filled them in on what the coroner had told him, and the letter Judy had left with a neighbor.

Buck couldn't hide his shock. Judy Ramsey was dead, murdered, and now it looked like Maribelle Brookshire was behind it. He was glad Willie hadn't broken the news to Ansley. He'd seen how happy she was to find her biological family.

"If true," he asked, "why would Maribelle Brookshire kill Judy? To keep Ansley from finding her. What was she afraid Judy might say? Even if the adoption wasn't legal, why add murder to your list of crimes?"

Willie swore. "How did Maribelle Brookshire even know about Judy Ramsey, let alone that she was having a baby? Judy was definitely involved in the illegal adoption. So where is Ansley's mother? They had to have known each other."

"Maribelle somehow knew Judy Ramsey, who knew Ansley's birth mother," Buck said. "She had to be the one Judy was buying the yarn and knitting book for."

"Judy got paid fifty thousand dollars for the transaction," James said.

He glanced at Tommy, who said, "I'm already on it. She never deposited the money in the bank so she must have gotten cash. If there was a money trail, I would have found it."

"That note isn't enough to arrest Maribelle Brookshire, though, is it," Buck said, realizing how hard it would be to get justice.

Willie shook his head. "We'd need a smoking gun to take on that family."

"I doubt Maribelle would have done it herself. Probably had Lanny Jackson do it," James said.

Buck had to disagree. "I've met her. I'd say she is capable of just about anything."

"I'm still dealing with Ansley being our half sister," Davy said. The celebratory mood from earlier was gone. Realization had set in. "How could Dad keep something like this from us?" The brothers exchanged looks.

"I've got some errands to run," Buck said, reaching for his Stetson and heading for the door. He knew they'd want to talk about this among themselves.

"WHY WOULD DAD have kept it from us?" Davy repeated after Buck left.

There was a general shaking of heads before Tommy said, "There's a chance he didn't know about her."

But Willie shook his head. "He knew. I was going to tell you… I found the jewelry store that did the engraving of the necklace from Dad's pickup. To have engraving done, you're required to sign a form with what you want printed on the item." He looked up. "Dad's phone number was on it. He bought the necklace with 'Del-Rae' engraved on it thirty years ago. If Ansley is right about her birth date, he bought it before she was born."

"So what happened?" Tommy demanded. "Why are we just learning about this now?"

"It wasn't like our father to keep secrets, was it?" James said.

The room fell silent again as if this last piece of evidence destroyed the last shred of doubt. Their father had known that he had a daughter.

Willie's cell phone rang. He checked the screen and

frowned as he said, "It's Buck," before picking up. "What do you mean, Ansley's missing? Hold on, I'm at the office. I'm putting you on speaker."

Buck's worried voice filled the room. "I just went by her motel room. Earlier we'd agreed to meet for lunch to celebrate the news. She's gone—didn't check out. A maid saw a man drive away in her car. The man's description matched that of Lanny Jackson."

Willie swore, looking at his brothers. "Pretty clear who's behind it. I'll let law enforcement in Bozeman know that she's missing. Let the law handle this, Buck. Don't do anything rash." He swore as Buck disconnected.

"Wherever Ansley is, she doesn't know about Judy Ramsey's murder or that she definitely isn't her birth mother," Tommy said.

"When I got James's call about the DNA report, I'd just learned that Judy wasn't the birth mother and about the letter naming Maribelle her killer," Willie said. "After finding out that Ansley is our sister, I figured the news could wait."

James tried her number. It went straight to voice mail. "Buck's right. She's in trouble. We have to find her."

"I'm headed to Bozeman and the Brookshires now," Willie said. "Keep looking for her birth mother. All of us storming Brookshire Estate isn't going to help. I would imagine Buck is already on his way there. I'm not sure who's in more trouble right now—Ansley or Buck."

BUCK DROVE TOO FAST. It would be just his luck to get picked up by one of the state highway patrol officers he used to work with. But traffic was light, as usual, and he reached Brookshire Estate in record time.

As he pulled in past the gate, he noticed the cameras again. It didn't matter, he told himself. They would know he was coming, anyway. He roared up the road, coming to a dust-boiling stop in front of the house. No one rushed out to stop him as he climbed out of his pickup and headed for the front door.

The same housekeeper answered the door as last time. "I want to see Maribelle Brookshire," he said, pushing past her.

"She isn't here," the woman said, chasing after him as he strode into the living room. "No one is here. The family has gone on vacation."

He swore as he spun on her. "Vacation? Where?" He could see she was about to say that she couldn't reveal where they'd gone. "Where?"

"I don't know. I honestly don't."

Buck was surprised, but he believed her. "Was Ansley with them?"

The woman hesitated but only for a moment. "I believe they were meeting her. That's all I know. Please, you should leave."

He glanced toward the stairs and considered searching the house. "What vehicle did they take?"

"Mrs. Brookshire took her SUV. I believe Mr. Brookshire was meeting her after work. His driver was taking him, I think."

"Did you see Ansley?"

She shook her head. "Please don't get me fired. I need this job."

"I won't." He headed for the door but stopped. "One

more question. Did Mr. Brookshire's bodyguard go with him?"

"I wouldn't know. I haven't seen Mr. Jackson."

Climbing back in his pickup, he considered where they might have gone. He didn't believe for a minute that Ansley had agreed to this, let alone that she was meeting them at their destination. She'd been taken. Why else was Lanny Jackson seen driving her SUV away from the motel?

Buck slammed his palm against the steering wheel. He'd known they were going to find out that her so-called adoption had been illegal. He just hadn't thought the Brookshires would go to this extreme to keep it from coming out. But he should have, he thought as he started the engine and drove back down the road.

He'd just turned out of the gate when he caught a flash of light off to his right. Before he could react, his side window exploded. His foot came off the gas as glass rained down on him.

Dazed from the impact, Buck watched, blurry-eyed, as Lanny Jackson reached in, unlocked his door, flung it open and shoved him over. He tried to reach for the gun in the holster at his back, but his movements were slow and awkward from the blows to his head. He barely felt the needle prick his shoulder. The lights dimmed and went out, but not before Buck saw Lanny climb behind the wheel of the pickup and a man he suspected was Gage Sheridan get behind the wheel of Lanny's black SUV.

ANSLEY OPENED HER eyes with a start. She'd been asleep? Must have, because in the nightmare, she'd been calling for help, but there was no one listening. She blinked, seeing what appeared to be a hospital room. No, this room was more sterile and apparently only furnished with a bed.

Her brain felt fuzzy as her eyes focused on a figure standing in the shadows. "Gage?" His name came out garbled. Her tongue felt too big for her mouth. She tried to sit up, but with a bolt of terror, she realized that she was strapped to the bed. Her eyes widened in horror as she fought the restraints.

"Don't," Gage said as he quickly moved to her. "You'll hurt yourself."

"What—" She tried to swallow, but her mouth was cotton. "Wha—"

"Water," he said. "Just relax. I'll get you some." He moved out of her view and returned a moment later with a paper cup. A bendy straw stuck out of it. He navigated the end to her mouth.

She drank, sucking down the lukewarm liquid as if she'd been lost in the desert for days. All the time, her gaze was on Gage as bits and pieces of memory began to come together. The moment he drew the cup back as it ran dry, she tried to speak again. "You lousy son of—"

"I did what I had to do," he said, talking over her.

"Where am I?" She looked around again, terrified she already knew.

"We just wanted you safe."

"We? You and my mother?" Her heart was racing. "Get these restraints off of me."

He took a step back. "I'm not sure that's a good idea. The doctor will be in soon. You need to calm down.

You've been acting…delusional. We were afraid you would hurt yourself."

"You and my mother were afraid I'd learn the truth about both of you," she said. "Believe me, I've learned enough to know I can't trust either of you." He moved toward the door. "Go, coward. You can't keep me here, and when I get out of here, you won't be able to hide. Not even Maribelle's money will protect her from what I'm going to do to her—and you."

"See, it's this kind of talk that's got you in here, for your own good."

She growled deep in her throat, and he hurriedly pulled open the door and rushed out. As the door clicked closed, her eyes filled with tears. She told herself that Buck would find her. Her half brothers, too. They wouldn't let her rot in here.

Ansley held on to that hope and tried, as Gage had said, to settle down. She would have to hide her anger if she had any hope of getting out of these restraints.

BUCK FELT HIMSELF begin to surface. He lay perfectly still, concentrating on his steady breathing and ignoring his blinding headache. He was on his side, lying in the remains of a building. He could hear two male voices. He recognized one of them. Lanny Jackson's. He was arguing with someone, someone with a more cultured accent, although rather whiny. Gage, he thought.

"All you have to do is keep an eye on him," Lanny was saying. "He isn't going to wake up for a while— not as hard as I hit him. Also, that drug should keep him under."

"But what do I do if he does wake up?"

He *was* awake. He could tell without opening his eyes that his wrists were bound in front of him. Zip ties. That was good, because anyone with a computer knew how to get out of them. He tested his legs. Not bound. Even better.

"Here, take this, Sheridan," Lanny was saying.

"I'm not going to shoot him!"

"He doesn't know that," Lanny snapped. "We just need to keep him here until we can get Ansley moved to somewhere safer. Take it, Gage. You want to get her back, don't you? Then do what I say. I won't be long."

Gage Sheridan must have taken the gun, because Buck heard footfalls, then a vehicle engine start up, the sound of gravel under tires and then a sound much closer. Gage had come into where Buck was lying on a crumbling floor, musty and moldy smelling, but he could feel fresh air on his face. Not that it mattered. From what Buck could tell, it was now just the two of them.

Ansley's fiancé moved closer.

Buck could hear him breathing hard, scared. He knew when he made his move, he needed to waste no time or effort. Gage had a gun, and he might be just stupid enough to pull the trigger without even realizing it.

He felt a finger poke in his side and didn't react. Another poke. Gage was right next to him, close. The time was now.

Buck rolled over, swinging out both legs at where he estimated Gage had been hunched down next to him. The man tried to get up before Buck kicked his legs out from under him. Too late. As expected, Gage pointed the gun at him as he started to go down.

But Buck was too fast for him, too trained in just this type of thing. He grabbed the gun, wrenched it from Gage's hand with both of his and kicked again. Gage fell on his rear as Buck launched himself to his feet. Tearing his wrists free of the zip ties, he swung the gun around to aim it at Gage, who was trying to crab crawl away.

"Don't shoot me!" Gage cried as Buck stepped closer. He placed a boot to Gage's chest, shoving him back and pushing the muzzle of the gun against the man's forehead as he warned him not to move.

"I'm only going to ask you once, so think long and hard about your answer," Buck said. "I can shoot you right here, or you can tell me the truth right now. Where is Ansley?"

Chapter Sixteen

James found himself pacing the office, anxious to hear from Buck. "Bella's asking a lot of questions about our mother," Tommy said. "Why don't I have any memory of her? She died right after Davy was born, so I can understand him not remembering her. But shouldn't I be able to? I've never really known anything about her." He looked from one to the other of his brothers. "I've never even seen a photo of her. Why did Dad never talk about her? Don't you think it's odd?"

"She was sick a lot and not around when we were growing up and then she died," Willie said.

"So we've been told, but that's about it," Davy said. "You must remember her." When Willie said nothing, he moved his gaze to James.

"She wasn't well," Willie said. "I was busy helping raise you bunch, so no, I don't remember much."

"Have we ever been to her grave?" Davy asked.

Willie shook his head. "I think Dad had her cremated. I was ten. I don't remember a funeral. I just know that Dad never wanted to talk about her."

"And about that same time Davy was conceived, he

knocked up some other woman?" Tommy demanded. "And kept that a secret, too?"

Willie got to his feet. "I don't have time for this. Ansley is our sister, DelRae. It's a fact. Let's deal in facts until we know the rest. Right now she's in trouble, and if I know Buck, he is, too." He walked out.

The air in the office felt thick and hard to breathe in the silence that followed. James broke it. "Buck will be fine." He had to believe that. "Ansley's birth mother is the key. We have to find her, and not just for our client. We have to know the truth. We need to know for certain if it was Penny Graves who borrowed that old pickup from Mark's lot. What's interesting is that her grandmother used to be a midwife. Didn't the grandmother have a cabin up in the mountains?"

"You think Penny could be Ansley's biological mother?" Tommy asked.

"If she is, then the cabin could be the perfect place to hide a pregnancy—and even have a baby you didn't want anyone to know about," James said.

AFTER BUCK TIED up Gage so he wouldn't be warning Lanny, he took the man's keys and cell phone and double-checked the address for the institution. Outside, he took his own pickup—missing side window and all.

He drove fast, still shocked at how far Ansley's adoptive parents would go—let alone her fiancé. Gage had confessed that it had been Harrison who'd had her committed. His heart pounded. Lanny had gone to the institution to move her to a "safer" place. He hated to think where that might be. That's why he had to get there and stop this abduction, no matter what he had to do. He called James to tell him where he was going and why.

"Why is it so loud?" James asked.

"I'm missing the driver's side window, thanks to Lanny Jackson." He didn't mention that he was still trying to overcome whatever drug the man had used on him as well.

"They put her in an institution?" his friend said when he told him the whole story. "I can leave now and meet you there."

"No, I'll handle it one way or another. Harrison got a judge to commit her. You might have to get me out of jail."

"There's something you need to know," James said. "Willie told me that Judy Ramsey left a letter that implicates Maribelle Brookshire. He's going down there to question her. This could be over soon."

Buck had his doubts about that. "I was at the house in Bozeman. Maribelle was gone, supposedly on vacation. I got the feeling she wasn't coming back. I'm almost to the institution. Wish me luck."

"Be careful. I don't want you risking your neck."

"Too late for that." It was his heart he was more worried about, Buck thought as he turned down a narrow road. Ahead he spotted a two-story white building. A black SUV was parked in front. He roared toward it, wondering how he was going to find Ansley—let alone get her away from here.

Even if he and Lanny were on better terms, Buck knew the man couldn't let him take Ansley without a fight. He hoped to avoid bloodshed but worried that there was a good chance it would come to that as he swung into the parking lot, coming to a stop next to Lanny Jackson's big black SUV.

As much as he wanted to go inside the facility guns blazing, he knew he'd be better off to wait out here in the parking lot. Lanny had said he was moving Ansley to somewhere safer, which meant harder to find. The way Buck had parked beside the big SUV, Lanny wouldn't see him at first when he brought Ansley out.

He'd never been good at waiting, but this time, it was the smart thing to do. He checked the weapon he'd taken from Gage and his own that he'd retrieved as he'd left the hog-tied fiancé. Then he removed his Stetson and waited.

Buck didn't have to wait long. From where he sat, he could see the side of the building through his window and the black SUV's. There was a garden with benches closed off by a short wrought iron fence. He saw Lanny first. He came out, looked around, then disappeared for a moment before he appeared again, this time with Ansley. Buck could tell at a glance that she was heavily medicated. She leaned into Lanny, the large bodyguard practically carrying her along the sidewalk to the gate. She slumped against him as he opened the gate and led her out, closing it behind them as they made their way toward his waiting SUV.

"Bastards," Buck said under his breath at the sight of Ansley, eyes half-closed as she stumbled along, dragging one leg behind her.

Lanny struggled to keep her upright as he approached the SUV to open a back door. He swore, clearly having trouble opening the door and not dropping Ansley. "They were supposed to make you compliant, not comatose."

Buck eased open his pickup door and jumped out. The SUV was blocking Lanny's view until he rounded the front of the vehicle, coming at the bodyguard from the back. But before he could reach him, Buck saw Ansley suddenly come alive. She kicked out, slamming a foot into the big man's ankle before she kneed him in the groin, dropping Lanny to his knees.

She saw Buck when he came up behind Lanny and smiled as Buck hit him hard in the back of the head with the butt of his gun. The man toppled over onto the asphalt. Buck rolled him under the SUV and looked up at Ansley.

"Nice to see you," she said, her eyes bright.

"You, too."

He reached for her, and she stepped into his arms. He could feel her trembling and didn't want to think about what she might have been through inside that place. He held her for a few moments, worried that Lanny would come to and try to stop them. He didn't want to shoot the man, but he would if he had to. "Let's get you out of here." He led her around to the passenger side of his pickup.

"I'm fine. I didn't take the pills they tried to give me," she said as she climbed in without any help. As he brushed his fingers over her arm, he realized she was trembling with rage. "This was Maribelle's doing," she said through gritted teeth. "I want to see her."

He closed the door, checked to make sure that Lanny

was still out and went around to climb behind the wheel. "Not a good idea. Harrison got a judge to commit you. All Maribelle has to do is make one phone call and you will be locked up again. As it was, Lanny was taking you to another institution, the next one more isolated, with more security. It sounded like they intended to keep you there indefinitely."

Tears filled her eyes, and she turned away. "All this because I wanted to find my birth mother?"

"Apparently so." There was so much he needed to tell her, and yet he hesitated. She'd been hit with enough. "I'm taking you to my family ranch. You'll be safe there."

He'd expected her to object, but all she did was nod and turn to glance out the side window. He could see that whatever had happened back there, it hadn't taken away her determination or her spirit. She just looked tired, beaten down—but only for the moment.

Buck was glad when she leaned back, closed her eyes and fell asleep.

IT WAS LATE by the time they reached the ranch. Ansley stirred when he lifted her out of the truck but didn't wake as he took her inside. He'd called to have his father make up the guest bedroom.

Wendell met them at the door, glancing at an exhausted Ansley, then at his son. Buck could see the worry in his eyes. Earlier he'd told him that it might be dangerous bringing her to the ranch, but his father hadn't hesitated.

"She'll be safe here," the rancher had said.

Buck carried her into the guest room, laid her down on the bed. She let out a sigh and rolled over. He studied the peaceful look on her face for a moment, then covered her with one of his mother's quilts, turned out the light and left the room. His father was waiting for him out on the porch.

"I'm sorry about this," Buck said as he sat down to look out at the darkness, wondering how much time they had before all hell broke loose.

"If the law comes, we'll handle it," Wendell said without looking at him.

"It won't be the law." The Brookshires had gotten the commitment order from a judge, but it was Lanny Jackson who did the real dirty work. He'd failed to get Ansley to another asylum. When Lanny came for them, he would be looking for vengeance this time. "The Brookshires will send their hired thug, Lanny Jackson." He described the man for his father. "He'll be looking for me to settle a score as well as take Ansley. I can't let him do that."

His father was silent for a long moment. "I assume the Colts are working through legal avenues to stop all this."

"The Brookshires have apparently left the country, but that won't stop Jackson. Even if they tried to call him off, he won't let this go."

Buck expected his father to ask him about Ansley, but maybe there was no reason. He'd brought the woman home to the ranch. Didn't that say it all about how involved he was with her? "I don't like you being here alone when Jackson comes looking for me."

"I won't be. Your brother gets back tomorrow with stock from the latest rodeo. He and the ranch hands will be more than enough. Don't discount your old man, either. I can still handle myself."

Buck smiled over at this father. "I'd never do that." He felt such love for this man who'd taught him so much about life.

"But we'll be leaving again in a few days for another rodeo," Wendell said.

"Lanny will make his move before then."

They were quiet for a few minutes. "Any closer to finding her mother?" his father asked.

He shook his head. "But we're not giving up."

"I figured as much." Wendell nodded, but the look in his eyes was one of worry as he went inside.

Buck sat for a few more minutes listening to the frogs down at the pond, the hoot of an owl in the distance, the sound of the wind in the nearby pines. He grew up with these sounds. They comforted him even when he knew trouble was coming. Still, he felt safer here than anywhere on earth.

Rising, he went inside to check on Ansley.

SHE WOKE TO DARKNESS, and for a moment she thought she was back at the institution. She let out a cry of anguish before she realized she was no longer strapped down. Sitting up, she shoved off the quilt, still disoriented as she frantically tried to see in the blackness. At the creak of a floorboard, she turned to find a large, dark figure standing in the doorway.

For just an instant, her breath caught in her throat and she felt her eyes go wild with terror.

"Ansley?" Buck quickly stepped into the room to turn on the small lamp next to her bed.

She blinked as the room came into focus. Buck. She was safe. Her memory came back—Buck carrying her in from the pickup. She'd been so exhausted but also fighting the drugs they'd injected her with while she was captive. Yet her heart was still thundering in her chest.

"You're safe," he said as he sat down on the edge of the bed. He reached for her, and she came to him, letting him gather her up again in his arms—the only place she felt safe.

"Buck," she whispered as she drew back to look into his eyes. He'd saved her from that horrible place. He'd saved her from Lanny. Also, from Gage. He'd saved her in so many ways. She felt such a surge of emotion. This cowboy, she thought, shocked by the raw, primal need she felt for him. It was beyond desire. She wanted this cowboy for keeps. "Buck."

Cupping his handsome face, she kissed him—at first tentatively and then with passion as he responded in kind. Her fingers worked at the snaps on his Western shirt, releasing one, then another until she could touch the bare skin of his chest.

She pulled back, frowning with surprise and concern as her fingers felt the rough edge of a long scar that ran diagonally from his breastbone down across his abdomen.

"It's a long story," he said.

"The woman who almost killed you."

He nodded.

Her heart ached for what he must have gone through. "I'm so glad she didn't," she said, then bent to leave a trail of kisses across the scar. He groaned and drew her closer to kiss her passionately, deepening the kiss and then pulling back to look at her in the glow of the bedside lamp.

She answered his questioning gaze by slowly beginning to unbutton her blouse. He rose to close and lock the door and was back before she reached the third button.

Later, lying in his arms, Ansley sighed. She'd never felt this sated, this content. She thought about how his hands, his mouth had explored her body. The touch of his tongue, the quickening of her heart as he bent to take her aching, rock-hard nipple between his teeth. Her legs had trembled as he'd stroked her to a height she'd never reached before.

She shivered at the memory of their lovemaking, and he pulled her closer, kissing her temple. "You can tell me," she said quietly. "I overheard Lanny talking to Gage, so I know a little."

He hesitated, but only for a moment. Ansley listened as he told her about Judy Ramsey being murdered, but that she definitely wasn't her birth mother. Then he told her about the letter Judy left and how Willie was meeting the local sheriff down in Gallatin County before they headed out to talk to Maribelle and Harrison.

She took it all in, sifting through the parts that hurt

to reach the news that buoyed her. "I was supposed to be named DelRae?"

"It seems so. After your father, Del Ransom Colt. Apparently, your birth mother made Judy Ramsey promise, and Judy made Maribelle promise."

She made a disgusted sound. "So like Maribelle to break that promise."

"Ansley, there is a good chance that Maribelle either killed Judy Ramsey or had her killed to keep her quiet. Now more than ever, your adoptive parents want you under lock and key. You have to trust that we're all still trying to find your birth mother and keep you—and her—safe."

"I trust you and my brothers," she said, her voice breaking. "But there isn't enough evidence to arrest Maribelle and Harrison, is there?"

He shook his head. He didn't have to tell her that the justice system was weighted toward those with money and power. "I believe both Lanny and Gage are getting their orders from Maribelle or Harrison. That's why I wanted you here, where I can keep you safe." He looked at her as if expecting her to argue.

Instead, she nodded. "I know now what they can do to me. That place... I was strapped down..." Tears welled again. She wiped at them furiously. "I want them to pay for this."

"If I'm right, Maribelle didn't know about the letter Judy left as insurance. It might not be enough to convict her, but it's a start. In the meantime, we might be getting closer to finding your birth mother."

"How, with Judy Ramsey dead?"

"James thinks the two of us need to talk to a woman named Penny Graves." She listened as he told her about what they'd learned and how it led back to city hall. "The one thing we know is that Judy knew your birth mother well enough that she was the one who brokered the deal with Maribelle," he said.

"Why the intermediary? Why wouldn't my mother make the deal?"

"Good question." He hesitated. "She might not have known what Judy was up to or that she was paid fifty thousand dollars."

"So that's what I was worth. Fifty grand?" Ansley said and shook her head. "That amount is nothing to Maribelle. She must have thought she got a real deal—until she realized her mistake. I was never the daughter she wanted."

"Her loss." He drew her close. This time they made love slowly. Ansley told herself that she never wanted to leave this bed—or this man.

But when she woke the next morning, she was alone. She rose, showered and went to find Buck. Not surprised to find him in the kitchen making pancakes. He poured her a cup of coffee as she sat down at the island.

All he had to do was smile at her, and she felt the heat rush again through her body. As she slipped her coffee, though, she knew this couldn't last. Lanny was still out there. He'd be coming after Buck—if not her—again. As for Gage… She pushed the thought of him away and thought instead about the woman who'd given birth to her.

Would she ever find her?

IT DIDN'T TAKE his deputies long to find the murder scene. Willie sent forensics out to the abandoned motel and café to see if they could find any evidence that Maribelle Brookshire had been there.

In the meantime, he decided he had time to stop by the city office and check on who had borrowed the old pickup from Mark's lot. James had called just as he was leaving the sheriff's department to tell him what Wendell Crawford had said about Del and Penny possibly having dated way back when.

"No way. Dad and Penny? Not a chance." But even as he said it, Willie had to agree with his brother. Del Ransom Colt was proving to his sons how little they knew about him. He glanced at the time as he entered the courthouse. Later today he would be meeting with the Gallatin County sheriff for a visit to Brookshire Estate to talk to Maribelle.

Penny Graves wasn't at her desk, so he stuck his head in the open door of the mayor's office. "Did I catch you at a bad time?"

"Willie!" Beth Conrad burst into a smile. "I was just going to call you. I have some great news. I just got confirmation from the railroad. We're getting crossing bars and lights. *Finally.* I wanted you and your brothers to be the first to know. It's been an uphill battle. But we finally won."

He knew how hard Beth had worked on it. "Thank you for doing that," Willie said. Not that it would bring back their father. But it might save a life in the future.

"I'm sorry it took so long. If only that rail crossing had crossing bars ten years ago…" Her blue eyes shone with emotion. "Anyway, I was thinking maybe we could have a ceremony in Del's name."

"I don't know. I can ask my brothers what they think."

"I know it's too little, too late."

"No, it's amazing that you got the railroad to finally act. Dad would have been happy. It might save someone else the same fate.

"While I'm here," Willie said. "I heard that someone from your office borrowed a pickup from Mark's used car lot. Would you know anything about that?"

She looked surprised. "I don't, but I'll look into it if it's important," Beth said. "I'll have to get back to you. I did send Penny out to the RR crossing to shoot a few photos. We want to do some before and after shots once the work begins."

"Any idea why she would borrow a truck from Mark's lot?"

"Now that I think about, Penny's been having car trouble with that rig of hers. I didn't remember that when I asked her to get the photos. She's good friends with Mark's wife."

Willie nodded. He needed to get to Bozeman. He was anxious to confront Maribelle Brookshire. He'd known better than go alone. Having the county sheriff and a few deputies with them would at least get her attention—if not get her to break down and confess. "Thanks, Beth, and thanks again for working so hard on the crossing. Also, the former sheriff told me that you put in a good word when I applied for deputy." He waited for her to say something. When she didn't, he said, "Thank you. Let me know what Penny says."

THEY'D FINISHED THEIR breakfast and Ansley had helped with loading the dishwasher when she heard the sound of tires on gravel and froze.

"It's just the Colt wives," Buck said, seeing her instant distress. "They're determined to help you find your mother."

Before she could reach the door, the women had piled out and were headed for the porch. Ansley stepped out, and they instantly surrounded her like a flock of geese in a protective huddle.

She realized how happy she was to see them as they entered the house.

"I'll be out at the barn," Buck said after greeting the women.

"We're all from here, and we know this town, this county," Lori said once they were in the living room and all seated.

"Also, we're women, and the PI agency is looking for a woman," Bella said. "We can find her while the men do what they can to keep you safe."

Ansley smiled. "Your husbands are all right with this?"

Bella seemed to give this some thought, making the others laugh. "I was thinking of us working behind the scenes...so to speak."

"If your mother was a local," Carla said, "then how was it that no one knew she was pregnant?"

"She could have hidden it," Bella said, glancing down at her own flat stomach. "At least for a while, but then she'd have to hide out until the baby was born."

"Having Judy Ramsey buy pink and blue yarn and knitting supplies isn't really hiding it," Ellie pointed out.

"She could have said she was making the blanket for a friend and didn't know the sex of the baby yet," Lori said, waving it off.

"That's if someone caught her knitting," Carla said. "Why the secrecy? Like Lori said, she could have said she was making it for a friend."

"For some reason, she didn't want anyone to know she was pregnant," Ansley agreed.

"Because she was married to someone else?" Bella cut in.

"Or because a pregnancy would have cost the woman her job?" Lori said.

"That's a thought. Or just cost her her reputation?" Ellie said.

"Whatever the reason for keeping it secret, isn't it more likely that if her intent was to give up the baby, she would have gone away, had the baby there and returned without the infant? She might have been gone only a few months if she was able to hide her pregnancy."

"So why make the baby blanket if she had no intention of keeping me?" Ansley asked.

"Something changed," Lori said. "She wanted to keep you but couldn't. That's why she made you the blanket, to let you know that she loved you."

"Okay," Bella said. "If she went away, then that would have been noticed—even for a few months. With all the busybodies we have in town, someone had to have speculated, especially if your mother was a long-time resident."

"You're leaving out a key part," Carla said. "The father of the baby, Del Colt. Nearly thirty years ago, his wife was having Davy about the time Ansley's mother was having her."

"No getting around it," Bella said. "Del impregnated his wife at about the same time as Ansley's mother."

"According to my husband, Del wasn't that kind of man," Lori said.

As they talked, Ansley realized that she knew little about her father except that he'd rodeoed, quit to start the investigative business and died in a train accident ten years ago. She recalled the photograph she'd seen of him at the office.

But she told herself that she would get to know him through her brothers—and her birth mother.

"What we're missing here," Ellie said, "is our husbands' mother. Why is it we know so little about her?" They all nodded in agreement.

All Ansley knew was that Mary Jo and Del had married young and she'd died young, leaving Del with four rambunctious boys to raise alone. There'd been no other woman in Del's life—that the brothers knew of, anyway. Ansley wanted to believe that Del had cared about her mother, even loved her. But if her birth mother and Del Colt had been in love, then how was it that no one knew about them—let alone that the child they created was given up for adoption? No wonder James, and probably the other Colts, too, didn't want to believe their father would have given up his own child to keep his affair—if that's what it had been—secret.

"What do you know about Del's wife?" Bella asked Lori, who shook her head.

"James said he really doesn't remember his mother."

"Same with Tommy," Bella said.

"And Davy, obviously because she died soon after his birth," Carla said.

"Willie's the only one who must remember her," Ellie added. "But he doesn't seem to. As the oldest, he would have been ten when she died. Anyone know what caused her death?"

There was a general shaking of heads. "That's odd, isn't it?" Bella said.

"Makes me think there is more to the story," Ellie said. "All Willie has said is that Del raised them from the time they were little. I guess their mother was always sickly. Willie said he thinks his mother was in the hospital most of that time. He hates to talk about any of this. He just knows that she wasn't around. I suspect the pregnancy with Davy wasn't planned, since she died not long after giving birth."

The room grew quiet for a few minutes. "So there could have been another woman in Del's life," Bella said to Ansley. "If you're twenty-eight, born on the Fourth of July, then Del must have been with your mother about the same time Davy was conceived. But that doesn't mean they hadn't known each other, hadn't been in love, but that Del couldn't leave his sick wife."

They all grew quiet. "He already had three young boys and another one on the way," Ansley said. "I wouldn't imagine he would have wanted another child."

"I think we need to find out what happened to our

husbands' mother," Bella said. "I've never even seen a photo of her. Isn't that odd? Lots of photos of the boys growing up, but none of her with them."

"That is odd," Lori agreed. "Do we even know her name?"

"Mary Jo. I got that much out of Willie. I think he knows more than he's willing to share out of loyalty," Ellie said. "That alone makes me think something was very wrong with that marriage."

"We started talking about how to find Ansley's mother," Bella said. "But I suspect that once we know Mary Jo's story, it will lead us to Ansley's birth mother." There was general agreement.

How to do it, however, was debatable. But Ansley loved that these women wanted to help her. She really did feel part of the family.

The conversation turned to how she was doing and finally to Buck.

"He seems to have put some color in your cheeks," Bella said and chuckled.

"He was looking pretty happy before he headed to the barn," Lori said, and they all laughed. "We couldn't be happier for the two of you."

Ansley tried to tell them that it wasn't like that. "We barely know each other." But the women all giggled.

"We know Buck," Bella said. "Trust us. This is serious."

Chapter Seventeen

"They're going to come for her again," Buck said when he made the call to James from the barn. "I have her out here at the ranch."

"Not sure you having Ansley at the ranch is a good idea. If a judge really did have her committed, then what you've done is against the law. But you know we'll have your back."

"I doubt they'll go the legal route. I suspect they'll send Lanny Jackson. Hell, he'll be looking for me even if they don't send him to get Ansley."

"I don't like you having a target on your back," James said. "When I asked you to work with us—"

"It was my choice. We never knew it would go this far, but now it has. I can keep her safe here better than anywhere else. With the Brookshire money and power, there is no place safe for her right now except as far away from them as possible. I'll do whatever I have to in order to protect her."

"I know you will."

Buck broke the silence. "I probably should warn you that all the wives are out here. They're determined to help find her birth mother."

James groaned. "Lori already warned me. By the way, Willie called to say that he spoke to the mayor. She said her assistant, Penny Graves, might have borrowed the pickup from Mark's lot as we were told. Apparently she was having trouble with her car. Any chance it's not the same pickup?"

"None," Buck said and told James what his father had told him about Del dating Penny Graves. "Wendell saw them together. He said he thought their relationship had been contentious."

"Penny and my father?" James sounded as disbelieving as Buck himself had. "But you know, the way things have been going, why not? If I've learned anything, it was that I didn't know my father."

WILLIE HAD A bad feeling even before the housekeeper opened the door at the Brookshire Estate. He and the other law officers with him flashed their badges. If the woman who'd answered the door was surprised, she didn't show it.

"We're here to see Maribelle Brookshire," the Gallatin County sheriff said.

"She's not here," Ingrid said. "She and Mr. Brookshire have left for a vacation abroad."

"Then you won't mind if we have a look around," Willie said and handed her the warrant. That didn't faze the woman, either, as she took the warrant and, without looking at it, allowed them to enter.

It took a while to search the place. When they finished, they found the housekeeper sitting on a chair near the front door waiting.

"Do you know where your employers went abroad?" the local sheriff asked.

"I'm afraid not," the woman said. "Nor do I expect to hear from them until they call to tell me to get the house ready."

"When they call, I need you to call me," the Gallatin County sheriff said and handed her his card.

"It could be a while. I got the impression it would be a long holiday," Ingrid said.

Willie swore as he left the estate. Maribelle and Harrison had made a run for it. The local sheriff promised to let him know if he found out where they'd gone. Not that it would do any good, since at this point, Maribelle was only wanted for questioning. But once Lanny Jackson was picked up for abducting Buck, there was always the chance that he might enlighten them for a lesser sentence.

As Willie drove back to Lonesome, he told himself that finding Judy Ramsey's killer would have to wait. In the meantime, his brothers were still looking for the woman allegedly seen throwing something at their father in front of a bar downtown—just before he left in his truck and was struck and killed by a train.

Willie had tried once before to get information out of the former sheriff, Otis Osterman, without any luck. But as he neared Lonesome, he pulled off down a road by the river, determined to give it one more try—for their father's only daughter's sake. If Otis knew who the woman was, Willie was going to get it out of him.

Otis lived in a small shack-like cabin on the river where he'd retired after being sheriff for years. Willie parked and started to climb the steps that led up onto the porch. He could hear the whisper of the river off to his right, the sigh of the pines as the breeze moved restlessly through the trees around the cabin and the unmistakable sound of shells being jammed into a shotgun just before the double barrels were snapped closed.

"Mornin', Otis," Willie said as the grizzly old former sheriff stepped from the pines just below the front porch. His gray hair stuck out from his head. From the white whiskers covering the lower half of his face, he hadn't shaved in weeks—if not longer.

"You're trespassing," Otis said in a gravelly voice.

He flashed his badge. "I'm here on business. My office knows I came out here. Still thinking about shooting me?"

"Sure as hell is tempting," Otis said under this breath, but he lowered the shotgun. "What do you want? Make it quick. I got things to do."

"You've probably heard the news about my sister, Ansley Brookshire?"

The former sheriff nodded sagely. "You still looking for that woman seen arguing with your father that night? Suppose you think that's the birth mother. Just like I told you before, I got an anonymous phone call. Didn't see it myself. Can't tell you—"

"The caller? Man or woman?"

Otis sucked at something in his teeth for a moment. "Woman."

"She disguised her voice, because you know everyone in this county?"

The old former sheriff smiled at that remark, exposing several missing teeth. "She tried."

"Who called, Otis?"

"No one reliable, so I had no reason to—"

"Who?"

"Cora Brooks."

Willie swore under his breath.

"See why I paid it little mind? So your father had an argument with some woman on the street in front of a bar. All that proved was that he was in no shape when he started across that railroad track."

Turning, Willie walked away. "Next time you come out here," Otis called after him, "at least bring a six-pack, or better yet, a bottle of whiskey. Your father would have."

Willie called James. He needed to get back to the office. Mostly, he wasn't up to interviewing Cora Brooks. Not today.

CORA BROOKS HAD a reputation in the county for butting into other people's business. Usually it involved a pair of binoculars and a prying disposition. Putting her nose in places it didn't involve had gotten her house burned down some time ago. Since then she'd moved one of those tiny houses that had gained popularity onto her property.

As he drove into her yard, he saw that this house had a balcony on its third floor, making the place resemble a shoe. The old woman who lived in the shoe opened the door before he could even get out of his SUV. She had a shotgun in the crook of her arm but smiled when she saw him.

"Jimmy D," she called out in a voice both irritatingly harsh and high.

"I go by James now."

She laughed at that, a sound like fingernails down a blackboard. "You're still a Colt. Can't hide from that." She appeared older, frailer and maybe a little more hunched over, but he knew she was still as sharp as that tongue of hers.

"I would imagine you know why I'm here," he said. "What's it going to cost me to find out what you saw the night my father died?"

"Sure took you long enough to come to me," she said and eyed him, as if calculating in her mind what she could get out of him.

Cora set down the end of the stock and leaned on the shotgun. "That woman who hired you, the one staying at the motel, she's one of yourn, isn't she?"

He didn't bother to answer, figuring if Cora knew, then the whole county did by now. "Was the woman that night in front of the bar the woman she's looking for?"

"You mean the woman who born her?"

James waited, thinking about all the times he and his brothers had caught Cora spying on them. She owned a small strip of land next to their ranch. They used to steal apples off her trees. When they were really little, she'd shoo them away with a broom. After that it was rock salt from her shotgun.

"You know Penny Graves?" Cora asked.

He nodded. The mayor's assistant's name just kept

coming up. He felt his heart beat a little faster. Penny's grandmother had been a midwife years ago. Penny had borrowed the pickup from Mark's lot to do some business, allegedly for the mayor.

"You should talk to her," Cora said.

James considered the older woman. "You've known this all along?" He was surprised she hadn't come to him asking for money for the information. That was her usual MO. "Why now?"

She shrugged her narrow shoulders. "A girl should know her mother."

"Even if the mother doesn't want to be found?"

Cora met his gaze. "Who says she doesn't want to be found?"

"Then why hasn't *she* come forward?" he demanded. "She has to have heard that her daughter is looking for her."

"Guess you'll have to ask her that yourself," Cora said. "Now get off my property. I'd hate to have to call the law like in the old days." She smiled when she said it, though. "Never thought I'd see a Colt as a PI, let alone a sheriff. Guess I've lived too long." With that, she turned and went back inside her tiny house.

As he left, he glanced back to see her on the top balcony watching him drive away.

IT WAS LATE afternoon when James called. Buck and Ansley had been for a swim in the creek after the Colt wives had left. He'd told himself that he was just trying to keep her mind off everything. At least that was partly true.

James broke the news about Maribelle and Harrison having allegedly gone on vacation. "But I just got a call from Willie. They've both been picked up for questioning. They were trying to leave the country from a small airport back in New York. Also, we might be making progress on finding Ansley's mother. I talked to Cora. You know Penny Graves, right?"

Know probably wasn't the right word, but he said, "Yes?" He listened as his friend told him that he'd sent Davy up to check out her cabin. "It's secluded—great place to hide out. Might have even been a great place to have a baby. Davy looked through the windows and saw something interesting—a basket with yarn and knitting needles."

"Let me guess. Pink and blue yarn." Buck let out a low whistle and listened as James told him about his visit to Cora Brooks. "Sounds like we need to talk to Penny."

"If she's the birth mother, she might open up to you— if Ansley was with you. She'll be at work tomorrow, but after that she's going on vacation."

Buck swore under his breath. "That sounds like an ambush."

"It might not be Penny. You know Cora. She could just be yanking our chains. Knitting needles and even pink and blue yarn don't necessarily prove anything." But all trails seemed to have led to Penny. Of course, the trails had also once led to Judy Ramsey. As far as he knew, Penny and Judy traveled in very different circles. But then again, he'd have never expected Judy Ramsey's and Maribelle Brookshire's paths to ever cross, either.

"What is it?" Ansley asked as Buck disconnected.

He turned slowly to look at her. She'd been standing by the window looking out at the pine-covered mountains to the east but now waited expectantly. Her hair was still damp from their swim, her cheeks flushed from the sun. She couldn't have looked more beautiful.

Buck told her everything James had told him, including about Maribelle and Harrison being found and detained. "James thinks we should talk to Penny Graves."

"Who's Penny?" she asked.

He found it hard to describe her. Never married, Penny Graves was a slight woman who walked with a limp from a horseback accident. Buck remembered her coming to the rodeos out at the ranch. She was a woman who loved horseflesh. She was also a woman who could hide in the crowd—she blended in, had a way of going unnoticed. Had Del seen something in her that others didn't? Was that what had possibly attracted him to her?

"She's the mayor's assistant," he said. "Her grandmother was a midwife."

He knew James, Tommy and Davy were still working to find Ansley's birth mother, while Willie had put a BOLO out on the Brookshires. And still no sign of Lanny. Yet. Had Buck not been here with Ansley, he would have felt more anxious for answers. Even Ansley seemed at peace here on the ranch.

He liked this feeling of limbo, knowing that once she found her birth mother, she would be gone. As for Maribelle and Harrison, they'd been found. Whether Maribelle would be arrested and stand trial for Judy Ramsey's murder, that was another story.

In the meantime… "James said we could catch Penny in her office tomorrow—before she leaves on vacation."

Ansley nodded. "Then that's what we'll do."

He smiled. "What do you say to a horseback ride? We can watch the sunset from my favorite place on the ranch."

"Let me get dressed. I'll meet you in the stables."

ANSLEY STEPPED INTO the shower. Her face felt flushed from the sun, from the kiss, from the sunset and Buck. She still couldn't believe everything that had happened. There were moments when she regretted going looking for her birth mother, because as Buck said, she'd kicked over an anthill. But she'd also met Buck. Had released a part of her that she hadn't known existed.

They'd ridden the horses up the mountain to a spot on the edge of a cliff where the pines opened up. He'd spread a blanket on the ground, and they'd watched the sunset far off to the west—then made love before riding back to the ranch house in the twilight.

Her whole body had tingled. She'd never made love outside in the aura of the setting sun. She'd never felt such passion, such emotion. This cowboy…how was she ever going to give him up? Their lives were miles apart. They'd both gone into this encounter knowing it was only temporary, hadn't they?

She stood under the hot spray, hating the thought of it being over. Buck had opened up a whole world to her that she'd never known, and her brothers were here and their wives, whom she adored.

As she stepped out of the shower and began to dry

off, she heard her cell phone ringing and hurried to answer it. "Hello?" She was half-afraid of who it would be, but saw Gage's number on the caller ID. She hadn't heard from him since the day he'd set her up to be abducted and taken to the institution. If she hadn't been strapped down, she would have gone for his throat.

"Don't hang up. It's about your mother."

"I was just thinking about you," she said. "Have you now decided to help me find my mother?"

Silence, then a sheepish, "Maribelle's been released from custody. She needs to see you." He rushed on. "She says she will tell you everything. She's flying back to Bozeman tomorrow. She feels terrible about everything," Gage rushed on. "She just wants to tell you herself what happened all those years ago. Ansley?"

She'd been looking out the window at the rolling foothills, the pine-covered mountain she'd ridden a horse up only hours ago. Gage had broken the spell. She wished she hadn't answered the call. But now that she had…

"I'll think about it and let her know."

As she disconnected, she debated telling Buck. He would try to talk her out of going or insist on going with her. She told herself she'd sleep on it and decide what to do in the morning. From the beginning, she'd wanted the truth from Maribelle, to hear it from her own lips. She needed the whole story before she could put that part behind her.

BUCK WOKE TO the distant sound of a dog barking. His dad had taken his dog with him. He lay perfectly still in the darkness, his arm around Ansley, as he listened. He recognized the bark. A neighboring rancher's dog often wandered over into their yard after chasing a rabbit or a fox or even a deer.

He carefully removed his arm from around Ansley. She sighed in her sleep and rolled over. He waited to make sure she was still asleep before he slipped out of bed, pulled on his jeans and padded out into the living room.

The night was dark, clouds low, no stars. He thought he could smell rain on the air as he picked up the loaded shotgun and opened the front door. The worn wood of the porch felt cold on his bare feet as he eased out, then stopped to listen.

He could no longer hear the dog. Closer, the wind sighed in the pine boughs. Nothing moved. Until it did.

Lanny Jackson sprang out of the darkness from the right side of the porch. Buck swung the shotgun, but not quick enough. He felt something cold and hard strike his temple. The blow staggered him, but he didn't go down. Fighting blacking out from the blow, he heard the tire iron fall to the porch floor as Lanny grappled for the shotgun.

"I'm going to kill you, you cocky cowboy bastard," the bodyguard growled, so close Buck could smell the man's rancid breath. Lanny was strong and filled with fury for the other times they'd crossed paths.

Buck had let his guard down the past few days, having expected Lanny to make his move right away, since he didn't seem like the patient kind. Because of that miscalculation, Buck had thought with the cops after Maribelle, Lanny had taken off for the hills.

He'd been wrong, and it was about to cost him his life. Yet all he could think about was Ansley.

ANSLEY WOKE, sitting straight up in bed. At first she didn't know what had awakened her, until she realized it had been the sound of a gunshot. She looked to the other side of the bed as fear stole her breath. No Buck.

Hurrying, she sprang from the bed, throwing on clothes as she frantically tried to think of what to do. The bedroom door stood open. She saw no lights on in the house as she padded out. "Buck?"

She heard a commotion toward the front of the house. Through the sheer curtains, she could see the shapes of two men struggling for what appeared to be a shotgun. Buck and Lanny?

Her cell phone was back by the bed, but it wouldn't do any good to call for help. No one could get out here in time. What she needed was a weapon. She rushed into the kitchen. Even in the dark she could make out the hanging pots and skillets. But it was the block of knives that she raced for, picking the largest one and rushing toward the front door.

She'd barely reached the door when she heard the second shotgun blast. Throwing open the door, she lunged out. Shotgun in hand, Lanny was standing over Buck, who was bleeding on the porch floorboards. Her heart a thunder, she saw him put the barrel to Buck's head.

After that, everything happened so fast. With no thought but to stop Lanny, she rushed across the floor, knife raised. The bodyguard must have heard the door being thrown open. He started to turn, but by then she was already bringing the knife down, catching him in the side as he turned toward her. He let out a howl, swinging the shotgun in her direction with one hand as he pulled out the knife with the other. She heard the knife clatter to the porch floor.

She didn't see the barrel of the shotgun swinging toward her until it clipped the side of her head, dropping her to her knees. She thought Lanny would shoot her, too, but her heart was so filled with regret over what he'd done to Buck that she felt no fear as he towered over her.

"I should have killed you a long time ago," Lanny said. "Harrison told me that if institutionalizing you didn't work, I was to take care of you. That's right— your own father."

"He's not my father," she spat at him as she saw Buck push himself awkwardly to his feet behind Lanny. He had the fallen knife in his hand, and then he was driving the blade into the bodyguard's back.

Lanny let out another howl of pain as the shotgun fell from his hands. He staggered a step and fell to the side, knocking over a porch chair as he went down.

Ansley scrambled to her feet and rushed to Buck in time to catch him in her arms before he collapsed to the floor.

Chapter Eighteen

Willie left his brothers at the hospital. Buck had come out of surgery. The doctor said if he regained consciousness, he would survive. Ansley had been by his bedside and refused to leave since they'd been brought in.

"Let her stay," he'd told the doctor. "What can it hurt?"

As he climbed into his patrol SUV, he slammed his fist into the steering wheel. He couldn't remember ever being this angry. Maribelle and Harrison had been picked up at a private airport attempting to leave the country, but both had already been released.

The Gallatin County sheriff said that they didn't have enough to hold them without more evidence. The Brookshires were both going to get away with murder and so much more unless Willie could find more proof.

He sat for a moment, trying to calm down. He couldn't let this go. Judy Ramsey had been murdered on his watch. If nothing else, he would put the fear of God into Maribelle Brookshire. He started his patrol SUV and raced by the sheriff's office to pick up what he needed before he headed for the Brookshire Estate.

When the housekeeper answered the door, he pushed his way in. Maribelle didn't seem surprised to see him. She was sitting in a large leather chair in front of a crackling fire having a drink. She didn't move as he stormed in.

Pulling out the copy of Judy Ramsey's letter, he thrust it into her face.

"I know you killed her," he said. "She left a letter saying that if anything happened to her, you were the one who killed her. This proves you did it."

"What kind of foolishness is this?" she demanded after barely glancing at the paper before balling it up and throwing it into the fire.

"You do realize that isn't the original, right?"

The woman picked up her drink. "If you had proof, I would have been arrested instead of just being questioned. You should leave. If I call my husband..."

"I think you should call your husband, Mrs. Brookshire, because this isn't over. A woman was murdered, and she named you her murderer. I'll be back, only next time, you'll be doing a perp walk to my patrol car. If it's the last thing I do, I'll see you behind bars." He tipped his Stetson and walked out. Behind him, he heard swearing and things breaking.

He'd upset her but had accomplished little else. He had no evidence. He didn't even have proof that the two women had ever met. No way would this case get near a courtroom without a hell of a lot more.

Willie called home. After he told Ellie what he'd done, she chuckled and said, "Feel better?"

"A little." He smiled at just the sound of his wife's

voice. How he loved this woman. She kept him centered. "I'm on my way home."

"Drive careful."

"Any word on Buck?"

"The same. We're all praying for him," Ellie said. "He's strong like the lot of you Colts. He'll pull through."

Willie sure hoped so. He felt as if he and his brothers had gotten Buck into this mess. His cell phone rang. He saw it was Ansley and quickly picked up. "Tell me Buck is awake."

"Sorry," she said. "The doctor says there is nothing any of us can do but let his body heal and pray. But there is something I can do until he wakes up. I need your help."

"I WASN'T SURE you would come," Maribelle said when she opened the door to Ansley the next afternoon.

"Where's Ingrid?" she asked as she stepped inside, feeling goose bumps rise on her arms. The house felt too empty, too quiet. Ansley couldn't help questioning if this had been a mistake. All she'd been able to think about since last night was Buck. But as the doctor who'd performed the surgery had said, there was nothing she could do for him. He'd promised to notify her the moment Buck regained consciousness.

"Gage said you were finally going to tell me the truth," she said as Maribelle closed the door, locking them both alone inside this huge house.

"I'm so glad you and Gage are talking," the woman she'd believed was her mother said as she motioned toward the living room. "He's a fine young man. I hope you give him another chance. Would you like a drink? I could really use one."

"I'm fine," she said as she watched Maribelle go to the bar and pour herself a stiff drink. Was it possible she hadn't heard about Lanny's death after he'd tried to kill her and Buck? Or about Buck being in a coma in the hospital? No, more than likely, she was merely ignoring it, determined that Ansley would marry Gage and everything would go back to Brookshire normal.

"I know I handled things badly," Maribelle was saying. "I should have told you the truth from the beginning and saved us all a lot of trouble." She sounded too cheerful. It put Ansley's nerves on edge as she moved to the couch but didn't sit until she heard Maribelle behind her.

"When I called, you said you would tell me the truth if I came to see you," she said. "I'm waiting."

Maribelle made a disappointed face. "At least sit down. Please."

Ansley waited until the woman sat before she moved to sit closer to her. "I've waited my whole life to hear this," she said in answer to Maribelle's raised-brow questioning look. "But the moment you start lying to me again, I'm walking out of here, and I won't be back."

"Fine."

"You bought me from Judy Ramsey. Why don't you start there. How did you even meet the woman? You didn't live in the same town, let alone travel in the same circles."

Maribelle took a slug of her drink. "She was working for the caterer at a party I attended. I just happened to hear her throwing up in the ladies' room. I asked if she was pregnant. She said she was. I wanted a daughter so badly, so I asked if she was having a girl. She said she was. And that was that. We agreed on a price. It was impulsive. I knew nothing about the woman. Harrison would have had a fit if he'd known where I got you from, which is why I didn't want you finding your birth mother." She took another healthy drink of her cocktail.

"So you bought me from Judy Ramsey for fifty thousand dollars," Ansley said.

"I would have paid any price. I ached for a daughter." Her face fell. "Turns out I probably wasn't mother material. But I guess I don't have to tell you that."

She couldn't help but wonder why Maribelle was being so open, so candid. "I appreciate you telling me the truth. So you were worried that I'd find out that Judy Ramsey was my mother? Were you worried she would ask for more money? Or that she'd tell me everything?"

"Well, she'd kept our secret for more than twenty-eight years," Maribelle said. "But when you were so determined to find her, I feared she would weaken. Harrison couldn't know about any of it. I'm sure you can understand. He makes allowances for me, but if something like this came out…"

Ansley stared at her. Maribelle still thought the baby had been Judy's. "I get it. That's why you had to kill her."

Maribelle looked up, and their gazes met before she finished her drink and rose to pour herself another one.

"You killed the wrong woman."

Swinging around too quickly, Maribelle sloshed booze onto the carpet. "What are you talking about?"

"Judy Ramsey wasn't my birth mother."

"You're mistaken." She sounded confused, thrown off balance. One hand held the newly poured drink; the other grabbed the edge of the bar to steady herself. "If anyone should know, I should."

"Judy Ramsey tricked you. She must have lost whatever baby she thought she was carrying or had never been pregnant at all, because the coroner said she'd never given birth. Nor did her DNA match mine."

Maribelle's eyes widened, fear suddenly in her eyes. "That's not possible. If you're not Judy's, then... Where did Judy get you?"

"She played you right to the end, letting you believe that only the two of you knew your secret. There's someone else out there who can expose you and what you did, and you don't even know who it is. Probably won't until she shows up at your trial to testify."

Ansley tried not to take satisfaction in seeing Maribelle stumble to her chair and sit down heavily, clearly shaken. She reminded herself that the woman was probably at least partially responsible for Buck being in the hospital.

"You're lying," Maribelle said, but with little conviction.

"You should have gotten the truth out of Judy before you killed her. Too late now."

"She was mumbling something about insurance, but I thought..."

Ansley nodded. "She wrote it all down, everything about the arrangement you made with her and that if she died, you killed her."

"That ridiculous letter the sheriff tried to show me?" She scoffed.

"You thought she was just trying to stop you from pulling the trigger, right? Well, she did have insurance. But the real evidence against you will be my birth mother when she comes forward with what she knows."

Maribelle was shaking her head. "Judy swore that she didn't tell anyone."

"Was that before or after you shot her?"

"Stop saying that," the woman snapped, finally acting more like the mother Ansley had grown up with. "I did what I had to do. I did it for you as well as our family. If you had just listened to me and not gone looking for the woman, none of this would have happened. I wouldn't have been forced to shoot that bitch."

"Or have me institutionalized?"

"That was your own fault. You wouldn't listen to reason. If it wasn't for that cowboy, you'd still be locked up. I would have left you there until you came to your senses or until you rotted. You've always been a disappointment to me." She took a gulp of her drink.

"So you did tell Lanny to kill not just Buck but me as well."

Maribelle glared over at her. "I told Harrison that Lanny was worthless. I should have known he'd mess it up. Gage is right. You don't deserve being a Brookshire. When you find whoever gave you birth, change your name since you're dead to me. If Lanny wasn't such a screwup I would be at your funeral right now." She downed the rest of her drink. "Where do you think you're going?" she demanded as Ansley rose from her chair. "I wanted to see you because I need to make sure you're not going to keep turning over rocks looking for whoever did pop you out."

"I've heard enough," she said as she started for the door.

"You might as well sit back down. You aren't going anywhere. I knew I couldn't trust you. I knew I'd have to deal with you myself."

At the door, Ansley unlocked it before turning to face Maribelle—and the gun she was holding. "Do you really think you can get away with shooting me, too?"

"You underestimate me just like Judy Ramsey did," Maribelle said. "Harrison's new bodyguard will clean up the mess, just like Lanny cleaned up Judy Ramsey after I told him where to find what was left of her."

"You're that sure you can get away with murder again?"

Maribelle laughed. "I'll never go to prison. I'm too rich and Harrison is too powerful in this state. I can get away with murder. I already have."

"Probably not this time," Ansley said as the law enforcement officers rushed in, guns drawn, and quickly disarmed Maribelle. As they put on the handcuffs, she screamed that she'd only been trying to defend herself against Ansley, who'd come here to kill her.

"I hope you heard all of that," she said to Willie and the Gallatin County sheriff.

"Loud and clear," Willie said. "Are you all right?"

"I will be," she said as a female officer removed the wire. All she could think about was getting back to Lonesome. Buck was still unconscious. After a stop by the hospital, she was going to finish what she'd started.

Chapter Nineteen

The city offices were about to close when Ansley walked into the mayor's outer office. The name on the desk read Penny Graves. The woman behind the desk was just as Buck had described her. Penny instantly seemed flustered, making Ansley feel as if she'd come to the right place.

"I'm Ansley Brookshire," she said. "I'd like to talk to you about Del Colt."

Penny started to rise but then lowered herself back into her chair. "I don't have anything to say to you." She started to reach for her phone. "You need to leave."

"What I need is the truth. A lot of people have suffered because of this lie. Buck Crawford is in the hospital. The doctor doesn't know if he is going to make it because of me. Because I wanted so badly to find the woman who gave birth to me. Why is it such a secret that Judy Ramsey is now dead and Buck…" She heard a door open and turned to find a dark-haired woman standing in the doorway.

"Mayor Conrad, I was just about to call security," Penny said as she got to her feet. "I can handle this."

"That won't be necessary." The mayor stepped forward even as Penny tried to argue against it. She was tall, her hair chin length, her eyes blue. She held out her hand. "I'm Beth. You're right. We should have met a long time ago. Let's step into my office."

Ansley looked from the mayor to her assistant, who began to sob as she dropped back into her chair. She kept mumbling, "I'm sorry. I'm so sorry."

"It's all right, Penny," Beth Conrad said, putting a hand on her assistant's shoulder. "Everything is all right." Penny sobbed harder.

Chapter Twenty

"I don't know where to begin," the mayor said once she and Ansley were seated in her office, the door closed. Still, Ansley could hear the woman on the other side of the door crying. "Please excuse Penny. She was only trying to protect me."

"Protect you from me or the truth?"

Their gazes met and held. Tears filled Beth's eyes. "Both. When I heard that some young woman was in town looking for her birth mother, I never dreamed you were looking for me. I was told that you died at birth. That's what I've believed for the past almost thirty years until…" She glanced toward the door and the sound of the distressed woman on the other side.

Ansley shook her head. "I don't understand."

"Penny has been my best friend since we were kids. We're like sisters. She's always been there for me, running interference, watching my back, fighting my battles. She was there when I realized I was pregnant. I was twenty-three, on a break from law school, unmarried and in love with a man who I thought wasn't available."

"Del Colt."

She nodded. "I'd always loved him as far back as I can remember. He married young after falling for Mary Jo. It's understandable. There was something about her that was so appealing—at least for a while. They had Willie right away. I don't know how much you know about his marriage. He kept it from most people. Mary Jo wasn't well. The night I got pregnant, Del broke down and told me what he'd been going through for years. Mary Jo was bipolar. She was also an alcoholic. She would be fine, and then she would take off on a runner. Often he didn't know where she was for days. By the time he found her, she'd be in such bad shape that he'd have to hospitalize her until the next time."

Beth took a breath and seemed to steady herself. "Del loved her, but she was slowly killing him. We'd always been friends. I knew he cared about me. The night he called, he told me that he loved me and had for some time. Mary Jo had finally agreed to a divorce. As much as it broke his heart, he wanted a fresh start with me. He'd been raising the three boys pretty much alone. Mary Jo had no interest in them, but she didn't want to let Del go." She shook her head.

"What neither of us knew was that Mary Jo had purposely gone off the pill. After agreeing to the divorce, she'd begged for one last night together. She got pregnant with Davy even though her doctors had warned her she couldn't have another child without risking her life."

Ansley knew that she had died shortly after Davy was born.

"I saw what Del was going through after he found out about Mary Jo's pregnancy. We'd used protection that night, but I'd still gotten pregnant. I couldn't tell him for so many reasons. I confided in my best friend. Penny's grandmother was a midwife. She agreed to bring my baby into the world. I dropped out of law school when I started showing, and I went to Penny's family cabin up in the mountains. That's where you were born."

"How did Judy Ramsey get involved?"

"She followed Penny up at the cabin. She'd been in the drugstore when Penny picked up some prenatal vitamins for me. She just assumed Penny was the one who was pregnant. Judy and Penny had some kind of rivalry since grade school. Judy was planning to expose her."

Ansley groaned inwardly. "Or Judy had lost her baby or was never really pregnant but had already made a fifty-thousand dollar deal with my—with Maribelle Brookshire. Did she cut you in?"

The mayor flushed. "I had no idea that money was involved. The way Judy had explained it to Penny was that Maribelle couldn't have a child of her own and was desperate to adopt. By then, I knew I couldn't keep you and stay in Lonesome. I was deep in debt from college and what law school I'd managed to attend. I agreed to give you up because I wanted the best for you. I thought I was doing the right thing. But I have to tell you," she added quickly, "I wouldn't have done it had I known you lived. I would have kept you. I'm sure that's why Penny lied to me."

"You thought I died?"

"That's why when I heard you were in town looking for your birth mother, I knew you couldn't be looking for me.

"Apparently I barely survived a difficult delivery," the mayor continued. "Thank heavens Penny's grandmother was there and knew what she was doing. I lost a lot of blood, and for a while, I guess she feared they were going to lose me. When I came to, Penny told me the news."

"I'm sorry but how could you ever forgive Penny for lying to you like that?"

Beth's smile was rueful. "I asked for her help. She did what she thought was best. I think she knew that I never could have given up you or your brother had I known you both had survived."

"My brother?" Ansley asked, heart lodged in her throat.

"I'm sorry. I thought you knew. I was pregnant with twins."

Chapter Twenty-One

Buck opened his eyes to the very sight he'd hoped to see—Ansley. She smiled and moved quickly to his bedside.

"I am so glad to see those blue eyes," she said, her smile widening as tears filled her own eyes. She took his hand and squeezed it. "Welcome back. I've missed you."

"I was having a dream about you," he said, his voice rough. "I was worried I might never see you again."

"No chance of that," she said as she poured him a cup of water and helped him sit up a little to drink.

He took a sip, cleared his throat. "Lanny?"

She shook her head.

"I was hoping he'd live long enough to rat out Maribelle." Ansley smiled a smile he was becoming very familiar with. "What did you do?"

She told him about her visit to Brookshire Estate and how Willie had helped her along with the Gallatin County sheriff. "I was wearing a wire. I got her to admit to killing Judy Ramsey and much more."

Buck lay back, smiling at her. He'd thought he would never trust another woman. He hadn't met Ansley Brookshire, aka DelRae Colt, yet. "You are really something."

"I'm glad you think so."

"I feel like I've missed so much. Gage?"

"Holding Maribelle's hand, the ever-loyal almost son-in-law.

"But that's not the big news," Ansley said as she pulled up a chair. "I went to see Penny Graves." His eyes widened in alarm. "She isn't my biological mother."

"I'm sorry." He squeezed her hand. "Once I'm up and out of here—"

"Mayor Beth Conrad is."

"What?"

She nodded and told him about her visit to city hall. He had the feeling that she'd been leaving the best for last. She had that impish smile going again. "I'm going to need your help—and my brothers' as well. Beth was pregnant with twins."

Buck thought he'd misheard her. *"Twins.* Are you telling me there is another one of you out there?"

"Not quite. I have a brother. I haven't told anyone but you. I was hoping you'd get out of here and we could tell my other brothers together."

Lying back, Buck shook his head. "I don't know how to react to this news."

"It's great news. Penny swears my brother lived. The bad news is that Judy Ramsey told her she had someone who desperately wanted to raise him—a different buyer. Unfortunately, Judy took that information to her grave with her.

"Once you're out of here, I thought we'd tell the

Colts," Ansley said. "Not sure how they are going to take it."

"Yes, you are. Look how they welcomed you into the family."

"Beth wants to be there, as soon as you are well enough to leave the hospital."

"Beth and Del. That's makes so much more sense," Buck said.

"They were in love," Ansley said and smiled that smile he loved.

"Just like us," the cowboy said and pulled her down for a kiss.

ANSLEY HADN'T BEEN taking calls from Maribelle from jail. She'd been denied bail because she was a flight risk. Harrison had also been arrested as coconspirator. Both were awaiting trial for the killing of Judy Ramsey and for the attempted murder of Ansley and Buck Crawford. So Ansley wasn't surprised when it was Gage who called on Maribelle's behalf again.

"Your mother needs to see you," Gage said. "She's desperate."

"I'm sure she is. She's facing prison for her crimes."

"She's begging to see you," her former fiancé said. "Your father wants to see you as well."

Ansley thought of all the times that neither had wanted much to do with her. Now they both wanted to see her? "I'll see them," she said. She'd already been warned that her adoptive mother was behaving in a delusional manner, as if she didn't understand the gravity of the charges against her. Ansley hadn't known what to expect when she was led back into a room where her mother, wrists cuffed and attached to the table, was waiting.

"I'm so glad you stopped by," Maribelle said, brightening when she saw her, as if Ansley had stopped by the house for a visit—not the county jail, where she was awaiting trial. "I'm going to need something decent to wear to my upcoming hearing. I'm thinking the coral dress. It's always been lucky for me." She smiled. "Your father says I look good in it. You don't think it's too bright, do you? Definitely not the navy one. It's too drab for a courtroom. Makes me look like I have something to hide. Don't forget the shoes that go with the coral dress, and I'll need the handbag I always wear with it."

Ansley nodded as she took a chair across the table. She doubted her adoptive mother needed a handbag for her arraignment but didn't mention it. "Fine, but I need something from you."

Maribelle straightened regally. "Well, under the circumstances, I'm not sure how much help I can offer. Couldn't it wait until I get out of here?"

"What did you do with the other baby?"

"What other baby?" She looked genuinely perplexed.

"My mother gave birth to twins. A boy and a girl. You took the girl, me. What happened to my brother?"

Maribelle frowned. "How should I know? I paid for only one child, a daughter. I didn't even know there was another baby."

Ansley stared at her for a moment, then rose. "I assumed you wanted to see me because you would need clothes for your hearing. I brought the navy dress with some navy heels, because you do have something to hide."

Maribelle gave her an appalled look. "You're joking. I can't possibly wear that."

"I can get the coral one, with the matching shoes and handbag, but I'm not going to go get them until you tell me. What happened to my twin brother?" Her adoptive mother started to argue, but Ansley stopped her. "Otherwise you can wear the navy dress."

"Those aren't even the right shoes," Maribelle cried. "You're doing this to torment me."

"The truth. If I walk out that door, it won't be to get you the other dress. I'll put all your clothes in a dumpster."

She let out a horrified gasp. "Do you have any idea how much my wardrobe costs?" Ansley started to turn to leave. "Wait. My lawyer said there are going to be cameras in the courtroom. You don't want to do this to me. I'm embarrassed enough being locked up here."

"What happened to my twin?"

Chapter Twenty-Two

Once Buck was released from the hospital and back on his feet, they all gathered in the Colt Brothers main office. James had arranged chairs around his father's big desk, saying it felt appropriate to meet here. He'd had to borrow seats from the sandwich shop next door that Lori used to own so they could all sit.

Ansley had spearheaded the meeting. Beth had agreed to come and bring her best friend and assistant, Penny, with her. Buck had picked Ansley up. They'd arrived early, joining the brothers and their wives.

There was expectation in the air. Ansley couldn't help but think about her father, since he was why they were all crowded in his office tonight.

"Ansley wanted me to be the one to tell you everything," Beth began and told everyone the events that had changed so many people's lives. "I loved Del and, in turn, you boys. I don't know if you remember me babysitting when you were growing up. I tried to help Del when Mary Jo was…wasn't able. I would have done anything for your father. That's why after he told me that Mary Jo was pregnant, I kept my pregnancy from him. I knew he wouldn't leave her now. Then when she died, and your father was so filled with guilt… There was no reason to tell him and make things worse."

"But he must have found out," Willie said. "What about the necklace with DelRae's name on it?"

"Even though I'd decided to give up the babies, I wanted them to have something," Beth said. "I took up knitting. I was terrible at it, but I made each baby a blanket."

"The pink and blue yarn," Ansley said, her voice breaking. She looked at Penny. "So you sent the blue blanket with my twin brother?"

Penny nodded. "I'd also picked up a few clothes for each of them—you—down at the yarn shop. Beth wanted you to have clothes in case your adoptive parents weren't prepared, since you came early."

"That doesn't explain the necklace," Willie said.

"It's all my fault," Penny said. "I did something so stupid."

"No," Beth told her. "You did everything to help me." She looked at Willie. "I had the necklace made with the name DelRae on it and a bracelet with Del Junior, DJ, on it. It was silly and sentimental, but if I was going to give up the babies, I wanted them have something from me and their father. I had Penny order them at the closest jewelry shop. I had no idea that your father had ordered things from the same shop for Mary Jo over the years or that there would be a mix-up years later.

"If anyone is to blame, it's me," Beth said and swallowed. "After I lost the babies, I went back to law school, staying away from Lonesome out of shame. I'd heard that Del had quit the rodeo and started his own PI business. Davy had graduated from high school. All of you boys were rodeoing. I knew Del had to be so proud. I knew it was too late for us, but I needed to come home. I left the firm I'd been working for and moved my law practice to Lonesome. I had so many regrets and was terrified of seeing your father for fear he would see the truth, see my guilt, see my heartbreak and never forgive me for what I'd done. He was busy with his first big case, finding out who'd killed little Billy Sherman."

Beth took a breath before continuing. "I went up to the cabin where I'd spent some of the happiest and saddest time of my life. I found the necklace I'd had Penny make for my baby girl. But couldn't find the bracelet for my son. When I asked Penny—"

"I told her it was buried with him," Penny said. "Then she wanted to see their graves. I told her that they had grown over. I wasn't even sure where they were and that I'd gotten rid of the bracelet. It was supposed to have gone in the bag with the clothes and baby blanket that I gave Judy to give to the adoptive mother. I either missed it or it fell out. I put DJ's in his bag."

"How did my father get the necklace?" Willie asked.

"I stupidly took it back to the store where I'd bought it. I couldn't throw it away. It was gold. So silly. The clerk at the store called him, thinking he'd ordered it and just hadn't picked it up," Penny said. "Once Del found out I was the one who'd ordered it, he put two and two together..." She began to cry. "He confronted me outside the bar. He had the necklace and was demanding to know the truth."

"In front of the bar, the night he died," Willie said.

Penny dropped her head. "He handed me the necklace with DelRae engraved on it and demanded an explanation. I lied, told him yes, Beth had been pregnant, yes, I did order the necklace, but the baby died. He was heartbroken, desperate to find Beth. He kept saying, 'She was pregnant with my baby, with my daughter? How could she keep that from me? Where is she? I need to see Beth. This is all my fault.'"

Penny broke down for a moment. "I didn't know what to do. He was so upset. I'd promised Beth I would never tell. I had to tell him that she'd been pregnant. My heart was breaking, but the babies were gone." She shook her head, tears running down her face.

Beth put an arm around her and handed her a tissue. "Penny was only doing what I asked her to. What I thought was best for everyone at the time. If I could do it over…" She made a swipe at her own eyes. "But I can't."

"I've always believed that my father's death wasn't an accident," Willie said. "We've all wanted to believe that. We couldn't understand why he didn't see or hear the train or why he was on that road that night. The same road that led to Penny's cabin in the mountains."

"He was looking for me," Beth said, her voice breaking. "He was coming to find me. If he'd been in his right mind. If he'd seen the train…"

The room grew quiet for a few minutes.

"I tried to get Ansley to quit looking for Beth," Penny said. "I put that note under your motel room door, and I followed you in Mark's old pickup. I was just trying to protect Beth—and myself." She cried harder. "I never thought that Beth would ever find out that I went ahead with the adoptions. I thought it would be easier if she thought the babies had both died." She turned to Beth. "I'm so sorry."

"I know," Beth said drawing her friend close. "We all did what we thought was best at the time. No one wishes we'd done it differently more than me."

Ansley felt her heart break as the Colt women rose and went to comfort Beth and Penny. She joined them, thinking of how different all their lives could have been, but this was the way life had played out.

Beth drew Ansley close, both of them crying in both happiness at finding each other and regret for what could have been. Ansley would never know her father, but she'd found her mother—and her family.

She could feel the forgiveness filling Del Colt's PI office. His sons now knew the truth. Del had been trying to reach the woman he loved, filled with regret for all that they'd lost. Filled maybe, too, with what could have been. They would never know. Del would never know that he had a daughter who'd come looking for her family and found four brothers and their families, along with the woman who'd given her life. He would also never know that he had another son—a son Ansley would find—with the help of her family. They would all heal, because they would pull together, she thought as felt her brothers' arms come around her and Beth. Their love for Del and each other would always keep them together.

Chapter Twenty-Three

After everyone but the brothers had left, James pulled out the blackberry brandy. "We have to talk about this," he said. "Brandy before? Or after?"

Tommy grabbed the bottle from him and began to fill the small paper cups. "I, for one, am still in shock. I don't want to believe any of it."

But they all did believe it, James thought as he glanced at his older brother. "Did you know about our mother's...problems?"

Willie looked at his boots for a moment before taking a cup of brandy from his brother, but he didn't drink. "I was just a kid. But I knew something was wrong. Dad always seemed to be protective of me when she... wasn't herself, and then she'd be gone again. I never knew when she'd be back. But when she returned, they were happy. I was happy. She seemed best when she was pregnant, first with you, James. But after you were born, she was weird again and Dad didn't seem to trust her with a baby or a toddler, so she was gone again. Every time he had to take her away, he came back so sad." Willie took a drink of the brandy.

"That had to be hard for you," James said, but Willie only shrugged.

"The only thing that made Dad happy was the rodeo circuit," Willie continued. "I do remember Beth taking care of us sometimes when we were in Lonesome. Dad could have left us behind, but he wanted us with him on the road. There were always women around to take care of us. Probably buckle bunnies with a crush on our father. No wonder, though, that we all grew up loving the sights, sounds and smells of a rodeo. It was in us from the time we were born."

"Dad knew something was wrong with our mother, and yet they just kept having kids," Tommy said.

Willie took a drink before he said, "I think Dad hoped each time she returned that this would be the time she would make it. Also, she was happiest pregnant. But the last time she came back, when you were six, Tommy, I remembered them arguing. Then they seemed to make up, and I realized that she was pregnant again."

"That's when she'd agreed to the divorce, according to Beth," Davy said. "Don't you think Dad might have married Beth if our mother hadn't gotten pregnant with me?"

"None of that matters now," Willie said. "We got you, and we're okay with that."

Davy chuckled. "Why aren't we all more screwed up than we are?"

"Because we had Dad and we had each other," James said. "I remember Willie taking care of us, too. I know I could change diapers when I was three. Tommy was like a little mother to you, Davy. We were all protective of you."

"She died right after I was born?" he asked.

"Shortly afterward," Willie said and looked around the room. "It was an overdose. She got hold of some pills. I'm sure Dad blamed himself for that, too."

"How could we grow up with what had seemed like a normal childhood with all of this going on?" Tommy asked.

"Because, like I said, we had Dad and he loved us," James said.

"He let us run wild," Willie said.

Tommy laughed. "And somehow we all turned out okay."

"He must have really loved her." Davy finished his brandy and looked at his brothers. "But it sounds like he loved Beth, too, and now we have a sister by another mother."

"But Ansley's all Colt," Willie said, admiration in his voice. "She's the one who suggested wearing a wire to get evidence from a woman we knew was a killer…" He shook his head. "She's the reason Maribelle and Harrison Brookshire are facing prison."

"DelRae," Davy said. "DelRae Colt. Think she'll change her name? It will be like we're twins."

"Darned close," James said and room grew quiet.

"Might as well address the elephant in the room." Willie cleared his throat and reached for the brandy bottle. He began to refill each of their cups. "Not that I ever doubted it, but with the DNA results all back, we know that Beth Conrad and Dad conceived a daughter and another son. Penny swears that the son was born alive and that Judy Ramsey promised she'd found him a good home."

James saw the skeptical looks around the room. "Let's say she told the truth. Our half brother could be like Ansley and not even realize he was adopted, since we're all betting the adoption was done illegally. How would we even begin to find him?"

"I don't know," Willie said. "I just know that we have to. Ansley won't rest until we do, and neither will I." He glanced at his brothers and raised his cup. "To your next big case." They all drank and put the bottle away.

BUCK FOUND HIS father in the corral working with a green-broke yearling.

Climbing up onto the railing, he sat and watched his father doing what he loved most. It had always seemed strange to him that his father raised rough stock for rodeos but spent his free time breaking horses to ride. His father, like his grandfather, had made a good living providing stock for cowboys to try to ride, the rougher the better. Neither man had rodeoed. Buck himself had for a while, but he got tired of picking himself up from the dirt.

"How'd your meeting go in town?" his father asked without turning around. He wondered how long the man had known he'd been there.

"Fine."

Wendell Crawford turned from the horse to look at him and frowned. "Fine?"

Buck shrugged. "Got a minute?"

This made his father smile before he turned the horse back out to pasture and headed for the house. Margarita, a new addition to the Crawford household, met them as they reached the house. "Have a seat out here on the porch. I have peach coffee cake, fresh from the oven. I'll bring you both some if you're interested," she said as she wiped her hands on her apron and smiled at Wendell as he said they would be interested. "Coffee for you both?"

"I'd love some," Buck said and grinned at his father as he pulled up a chair on the porch.

"Don't say it." Wendell took a chair. Buck could see a slight flush to his father's face. He'd met Margarita at the post office, run into her at the grocery store and crossed paths yet again at the steak house one night. She was new to town, widowed and had been raised on a ranch. She loved horses.

His father had asked her out to the ranch, and over the weeks that followed, she'd given up the place she'd bought in town and moved onto the ranch. Buck had never seen his father happier.

"I like it," he said now to his father.

"You would. You're a damned romantic," Wendell said.

Buck laughed. "I guess I am. You know I'm going to marry Ansley."

His father nodded. "She's a beautiful woman. I like her. Think she'll be happy in Lonesome?"

"If you're trying to point out the obvious, I've got it. I have nothing to offer a woman like her."

"That's not true, Buck. And not what I'm saying at all." He shook his head. "You going to stay working with the Colt brothers?"

"Don't know. Maybe. Probably."

"What I know, son, is that you've never been interested in the rough stock business. Fortunately, your brother is. He wants to buy me out of the business. Got it into his head that I might want to spend more time traveling. I have no intention of going anywhere farther than town and back. My point is that this ranch is still yours, too. But if you want a house on it, you're going to have to build one."

Buck laughed. "I can do that. There's a spot by the river I'm partial to."

His father smiled. "I just want you to be happy—and not leave the land you love, even for the woman you love."

"Ansley knows me, Dad. That's why she's moving the design part of her jewelry business to Lonesome and opening a small gift shop."

Wendell nodded. "I've always figured it would take a special woman for you to ever trust again. I'm glad it's Ansley. She seems to have a head on her shoulders. That she's fallen for you tells me that she's one smart woman."

Margarita brought out the coffee and peach coffee cake and then excused herself.

Buck smiled at his father, amused. "What about you? A wedding in your future?"

"Eat your cake," Wendell said. "Your brother and I could lend a hand on that house you're going to build."

"Thanks," he said and took a bite of the cake. "Delicious cake, Margarita," he called back into the house as a white SUV came up the drive.

As Ansley parked and got out, Margarita said from the doorway, "Another coffee and more cake."

"Bring a piece out for yourself," his father said. "Buck and I have had our talk. Join us."

He heard a chuckle from inside the house as Ansley climbed the porch steps.

"Am I interrupting anything?" she asked, glancing at them suspiciously.

"Not a thing," his father said. "Not a thing."

"How's your mother?" Buck asked Ansley.

"Good. I can't believe that we now have time to get to know each other," she said. "We're so much alike." She laughed. "I used to dream of finding her, and now I have. But I never expected to find my family, let alone you."

"If you two are going to get mushy," Wendell said, pretending to rise from his chair. They shooed him back down. "Seriously, I'm happy for you both."

Later after the four of them had enjoyed cake and coffee on the porch, Margarita and his father went inside. Buck and Ansley helped clear up the dishes and came back out on the porch. They sat and talked as the sun set, taking the last of twilight with it. Buck took her hand. "Come on, I've got something I want to show you." Over their heads, stars had begun to pop out.

He walked her down by the river. "Have you ever seen a sky like that?"

She shook her head as she stared up at the stars filling the dark night from horizon to horizon. "It's beautiful."

"*You're* beautiful," he said, drawing her close. He

looked into her blue eyes in the starlight, remembering the first time. Fate had brought them together. Fate had delivered the woman he wanted to spend the rest of his life with. "I love you, Ansley Brookshire DelRae Colt Conrad."

She laughed, the happiest sound he thought he'd ever heard. "I love you, Buck Crawford."

"I know Beth wants to give you her name," he said, taking both of her hands in his. "So do I. I want to marry you, make babies with you, raise them here on this ranch. Does that sound like something you might be interested in?"

"Oh, Buck, I've never wanted anything more."

He grinned. "So you'll marry me?"

"Can we invite all of my family?"

"We are talking about the ones not behind bars, right?" She nodded. "Then I wouldn't have it any other way."

"There's just one thing," she said. "I want my twin there."

Buck nodded. "I had a feeling you'd say that." He pulled her to him. "We're going to have to find him, and quickly, because I can't wait to make you my bride and start working on those babies. I hear twins run in your family."

"Oh, Buck." She kissed him, promising a lifetime of love.

* * * * *

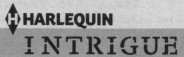
#2151 TARGETED IN SILVER CREEK
Silver Creek Lawmen: Second Generation • by Delores Fossen
A horrific shooting left pregnant artist Hanna Kendrick with no memory of
Deputy Jesse Ryland...nor the night their newborn son was conceived. But
when the gunman escapes prison and places Hannah back in his crosshairs,
only Jesse can keep his child and the woman he loves safe.

#2152 DISAPPEARANCE IN DREAD HOLLOW
Lookout Mountain Mysteries • by Debra Webb
A crime spree has rocked Sheriff Tara Norwood's quiet town. Her only lead
is a missing couple's young son...and the teacher she trusts. Deke Shepherd
vows to aid his ex's investigation and protect the boy. But when life-threatening
danger and unresolved romance collide, will the stakes be too high?

#2153 CONARD COUNTY: CODE ADAM
Conard County: The Next Generation • by Rachel Lee
Big city detective Valerie Brighton will risk everything to locate her
kidnapped niece. Even partner with lawman Guy Redwing, despite
reservations about his small-town detective skills. But with bullets flying and
time running out, Guy proves he's the only man capable of saving a child's
life...and Valerie's jaded heart.

#2154 THE EVIDENCE NEXT DOOR
Kansas City Crime Lab • by Julie Miller
Wounded warrior Grayson Malone has become the KCPD's most brilliant
criminologist. When his neighbor Allie Tate is targeted by a stalker, he doesn't
hesitate to help. But soon the threats take a terrorizing, psychological toll.
And Grayson must provide answers *and* protection to keep her alive.

#2155 OZARKS WITNESS PROTECTION
Arkansas Special Agents • by Maggie Wells
Targeted by her husband's killer, pregnant widow and heiress Kayla Powers
needs a protection plan—pronto. But 24/7 bodyguard duty challenges
Special Agent Ryan Hastings's security skills...and professional boundaries.
Then Kayla volunteers herself as bait to bring the elusive assassin to justice...

#2156 HUNTING A HOMETOWN KILLER
Shield of Honor • by *Shelly Bell*
FBI Special Agent Rhys Keller has tracked a serial killer to his small
mountain hometown—and Julia Harcourt's front door. Safeguarding his
world-renowned ex in close quarters resurrects long buried emotions. But
will their unexpected reunion end in the murderer's demise...or theirs?

Get 4 FREE REWARDS!

We'll send you 2 FREE Books plus 2 FREE Mystery Gifts.

FREE
Value Over
$20

Both the **Harlequin Intrigue®** and **Harlequin® Romantic Suspense** series feature compelling novels filled with heart-racing action-packed romance that will keep you on the edge of your seat.

HARLEQUIN
PLUS

Try the best multimedia subscription service for romance readers like you!

Read, Watch and Play.

Experience the easiest way to get the romance content you crave.

Start your **FREE TRIAL** at
<u>www.harlequinplus.com/freetrial</u>.